TAKING BACK LONDON

Katelyn Larson

This is a work of fiction. Names, characters, places, and incidents are either the product of the author's imagination or are used fictitiously, and any resemblance to actual persons, living or dead; events; or locales is entirely coincidental.

All Rights Reserved
Copyright © 2022 by Katelyn Larson

No part of this book may be reproduced or transmitted, downloaded, distributed, reverse engineered, or stored in or introduced into any information storage and retrieval system, in any form or by any means, including photocopying and recording, whether electronic or mechanical, now known or hereinafter invented without permission in writing from the publisher.

Dorrance Publishing Co
585 Alpha Drive
Suite 103
Pittsburgh, PA 15238
Visit our website at *www.dorrancebookstore.com*

ISBN: 978-1-6853-7404-4
eISBN: 978-1-6853-7548-5

TAKING BACK LONDON

There's always going to be people who tell you that you can't, but I'm telling you now, YOU CAN.

TABLE OF CONTENTS

Prologue: In the Beginning 1
Chapter One: Paris, France 3
Chapter Two: Outsmarting the King of Crime 8
Chapter Three: The Assignment 14
Chapter Four: The Speedy Getaway 19
Chapter Five: Adieu 28
Chapter Six: It was the Secretary, in the Office,
　　with the Letter Opener 32
Chapter Seven: Wanted: Dead or Alive 35
Chapter Eight: Ed the Shoemaker 41
Chapter Nine: Right Under My Nose 49
Chapter Ten: Spying on the Home Team 52
Chapter Eleven: NO DEAL 57
Chapter Twelve: Fast and Furious 61
Chapter Thirteen: Green with Gold Specks 65
Chapter Fourteen: Where in London is Justin Max? 68
Chapter Fifteen: Advice from Above and Below 71
Chapter Sixteen: Behind Enemy Lines 73
Chapter Seventeen: Slipping Up 75
Chapter Eighteen: Face of the Past 77
Chapter Nineteen: The Game of Truth 78
Chapter Twenty: Facing the Director 82
Chapter Twenty-One: Words Can Hurt You 85

Chapter Twenty-Two: Confessions 89
Chapter Twenty-Three: To Pull the Trigger
   or Jump 92
Chapter Twenty-Four: No Hope 95
Chapter Twenty-Five: You're Still in Love
   with My Sister! 98
Chapter Twenty-Six: The Hidden Cottage
   and Unexpected Guest 100
Chapter Twenty-Seven: Mark THE Almighty 104
Chapter Twenty-Eight: Alive and Kicking 105
Chapter Twenty-Nine: She's Dead?! 109
Chapter Thirty: One Down, Two to Go 111
Chapter Thirty-One: Denial and Suspense 115
Chapter Thirty-Two: Oh Shhh . . .
   and a Bunch of Other Words 116
Chapter Thirty-Three: False Truths 121
Chapter Thirty-Four: The British Are Coming! 123
Chapter Thirty-Five: Finished 126
Chapter Thirty-Six: The Foolish 129
Chapter Thirty-Seven: Backstage 132
Chapter Thirty-Eight: And the New Director is 135
Chapter Thirty-Nine: The Wake-Up Call 137
Chapter Forty: The One That Got Away 139

PROLOGUE: IN THE BEGINNING . . .

"Micky, I can't do what you ask! You've barely held your child and you want me to raise her?! ABSOLUTELY NOT! I'm about to be a mother myself, a single mother at that, and now you want me to take on two children at one time?! No!" Director Helen Austin of the MI6 AXL branch in London crossed her arms over her eight-months-pregnant round belly. Her married sister, Michelle Cameron, was sitting in a rocking chair next to her, smiling down at a three-day old baby girl in a pink blanket. She seemed unsurprised at her younger sister's outburst. Michelle kissed the baby's forehead before she responded.

"Edward will watch over her. Helen, words cannot express how hard this is for me; to let my child go. Edward and I discussed this many times before her birth, and we feel that you would be the best caretaker for our daughter."

"But . . ."

"Please, let me finish. Adoption papers have been drawn up. Ed and I will stage my death so Malcolm will think he's won. Please keep her safe, Helen," Michelle said; getting up from the chair to stand in front of her sister. Kissing her child's forehead one more time, she handed over her most precious thing in the world. Helen silently began to cry.

"Come now, quit that. You're making me tear up. Now listen to me very carefully," Helen stopped crying abruptly as Michelle continued, "My daughter will be one of the best MI6 agents the department will ever have. If Malcolm finds out who she is before she's ready to face him, it will be the end of London as we know it. But, if her identity is kept secret, she'll save London and rid the world of Malcom forever. Look after her and guide her. We're counting on you." Michelle gazed lovingly at her daughter one last time, took off her black moto jacket and tossed it on the rocking chair.

"This is hers when she graduates the academy," she said and turned to leave.

"Michelle! What's her name?" Michelle turned back with a slight smile.

"Elizabeth. Elizabeth Cameron."

"Cameron?! Are you crazy?! Why would you give her your own name? Won't Malcom know right away she's your child? Having your last name will give her away! And Michelle, how do you know? I mean, how do you know she's going to save London? How could you know? She's not even a week old!" Michelle just smiled before she walked out of her daughter's life.

This is where Elizabeth Cameron's story begins . . . twenty some years later . . .

CHAPTER ONE:
PARIS, FRANCE

He's late. Elizabeth Cameron thought, sipping her latte and taking a tiny bite of her chocolate chip muffin so she wouldn't get chocolate stuck in her teeth. Glancing at her watch, she saw that it was half past two and Louis Ward, her unreliable partner, was nowhere to be found. Sighing and reaching for the newspaper that was on the table in front of her, she looked around the small café.

Her waiter was behind the till, probably figuring her bill. The baker was behind the counter filling the display case with fresh pastries that were larger than her hand. *I should 've waited for one of those,* she thought, taking another sip of her latte and looking around again. A woman sitting at the table in front of her had answered her phone ten minutes ago and was having a fierce conversation with whoever was on the other end of the line. *I wouldn't want to be at the other end of her bark,* Elizabeth thought, turning her attention to the door of the café that had opened, and the cool end-of-April breeze brought in a tall, dark, and handsome man about her age, mid-twenties at least. He seated himself at a table in the front of the café, waved away the waiter as the man hurried over to him and instead opened a book, he'd brought with him, which appeared to be either a collection of poems or a novel of some kind, but she really didn't much care which book it happened to be. Elizabeth was gawking at his attractiveness with her mouth open when he happened to look in her direction. She could feel her cheeks burning as he gave her a smile and went back to his book. *Way to go, Elizabeth. He probably thinks you're a creeper for staring at him as you were.*

But, seriously, what a hottie. She thought as the waiter came over with her bill. Glancing at the receipt, she paid the full amount in cash. It hadn't been much food, but it was more of a meal than she'd consumed in the past week.

Zipping up her moto jacket, she stood up and made her way to the door. Just before pushing it open, she noticed that the hottie had shut his book and stood up very slowly; staring at her with the most mysterious look as she left the café. *Odd.* Once outside, she turned left to head to the second rendezvous point, where Louis would hopefully be waiting for her. Shoving her hands in the pockets of her jacket, Elizabeth prepared to take in the sights of Paris a bit, the people and the sounds. Her job rarely ever took her to Paris, and being as busy as she was, she really didn't do much else other than working and sleeping, when she could of course.

Getting an uneasy feeling, she looked up and down the street for signs of life but found none. *Where are all the people?!* Looking over her shoulder, she saw that the hottie was following her at a safe distance, but following, nonetheless. Quickening her pace, she slipped into an alley and darted into a small home that she found unlocked. After locking and bolting the door quietly, she unzipped her jacket and reached for her gun.

Surprisingly, she found no one home and as she paused to stand beside the front door after a thorough sweep, she wondered where the family might be. She suspected by the number of toys that were scattered about the floor that at least three small children lived there, probably all under the age of five. Hearing footsteps in the alley, Elizabeth quickly sidestepped around the toys and tiptoed up the stairs. *Thank goodness I wore my boots for this unplanned side trip.* She ducked into a child's bedroom that had a view of the street from the window. *This will have to do,* she thought as she put her gun away, locked the door and proceeded to barricade it. She pushed the bed, dresser, and for good measure, the child's heavy toy chest against the door; but only after she dumped the toys in the middle of the room and tossed them about. Finishing her ruckus and returning to the window, she found it was locked. Standing back to place her hands on her hips, she sighed. *Perfect for a child, but a problem for me.* Elizabeth went back over to the bed, tore the top sheet off the mattress and wrapped it around her hand. *Well, here goes nothing.* She closed her eyes and punched the window, shattering it to pieces. Taking the sheet off her hand, she was relieved to find she was not bleeding, and turned her focus back to the task at hand when she heard a commotion coming from downstairs.

Hearing many curse words in French, she shook her head. *The police must be after me too,* she thought as she glanced at her watch. The watch had a pink leather band that read the word READY as she heard a stampede of people coming up the stairs. She had one leg out when the police burst into the room.

"Stop right there, miss! We have you surrounded!" yelled a man with a thick accent that was more English than French. *Very strange indeed.*

"Not a chance," replied Elizabeth, as she slipped out the window and started to fall the short distance to the ground. Quickly turning in the air so if she landed on the pavement below, she would land on her back; she punched her watch arm to the sky and pressed the button that had started to glow RED on her watch. A grappling hook sprang out of the watch and caught the edge of the flat roof. The police had finally gotten around the toy mess she made and reached the window just as Elizabeth zoomed past them.

"Sorry boys, party's over," she called. Reaching the roof, she pulled herself up and quickly pressed the button that was now glowing GREEN on her watch and the grappling hook disappeared back into it. *Thank you, Ed,* she thought as she glanced up to look for a quick exit but was stopped dead in her tracks by the VERY REASON, she and Louis were in Paris to begin with. Standing mere feet from her was the man they needed to capture . . . again.

"On the contrary, the party has only just begun," he said with his thick British accent and before Elizabeth could react, the man shot her with a sleeping dart, and she dropped like a fly, unconscious and oblivious to what the world had in store for her. The man, who'd spoken to Elizabeth, went and stood by her body and smiled to himself as two tall muscular men came to stand beside him.

"What should we do with her now, boss?" asked one, reaching up to rub the hideous scar on his face, the scar that Elizabeth had in fact given to him herself.

"Take her back to London. I have something special in store for Elizabeth Cameron of MI6," the boss said as his phone rang.

"Well? Was she where I said she'd be?" asked an impatient British accented woman's voice.

"Yes, she was my dear, she was exactly where you said she was, and I do thank you for that, but you will have to excuse me, for I have an agent to torture, and you are using up all of my monthly minutes."

"What kind of crime boss has a set amount of cellular phone minutes?"

"The broke kind. Now if you will excuse me . . ."

"Don't forget about our deal! You promised!" whined the woman.

"Of course, my dear. Goodbye for now," the boss said as he hung up and rolled his eyes.

"Boys, we're London bound. And make sure you pay the pilot using the money from your paychecks last month," he finished, turning around to start walking to the rental helicopter that was behind them.

"Now wait a minute! That's not fair!" yelled the one with the scar on his face as he picked up the sleeping Agent Cameron as both men hurriedly followed their boss to the rental helicopter to head back to London; where another plan was forming at the hands of someone very close to Elizabeth, who hoped to end her future.

CHAPTER TWO:
OUTSMARTING THE KING OF CRIME

"I see you haven't changed since the last time we spoke, Elizabeth," said Malcolm Ferguson, the biggest crime boss in London, England; and literally a very round man himself. He watched struggling Elizabeth and smiled. For being the top MI6 agent in all of Europe, she was sure easy to capture. He had her tied to wooden rafters in an old, abandoned warehouse at the outskirts of London. She adorned a black eye and a nose that was bleeding again to go along with bruised ribs from the beatings Malcolm's thugs had been giving her . . . but, being kidnapped by Malcolm the month earlier when she was on assignment in Paris was exactly part of her plan; she'd just not figured on being in captivity this long. Struggling to catch her breath, she managed to answer the tall, very heavy-set man.

"I don't like change," said Elizabeth quietly with her head down. She slowly ceased her struggling. *What took him so long to show up? I could have been out of here half a month ago!*

"It's good that I do then," said Malcolm, nodding at his three henchmen, who pulled guns on Elizabeth.

"Wow, Malcolm! You're really moving up in the world! What happened to the old-fashioned way of doing things? What happened to throwing someone over the London Bridge?" said Elizabeth with sarcasm, twisting her wrists against the rope.

"I really out did myself this time, Elizabeth. I put some thought into how I was going to kill you for all the trouble you've caused me; although you're partly right on that last part. Your rotting corpse will be thrown over the bridge after I am finished with you. Once I kill you, I will be the top crime boss all over Europe and very soon, the world! Every criminal you have ever put behind bars will thank me because I killed you. But enough small talk! Any last words, Elizabeth Cameron, before I finish you off once and for all?" Elizabeth smiled at Malcolm before she answered him.

"Would you tell my mother that I love her . . . and eleven." Malcom smirked.

"I won't, unfortunately, be having that conversation with your mother . . . eleven? What are you talking about?"

"After we finish our little chat, it's going to take me eleven seconds to untie these ropes, knock out your three henchmen, take their weapons, put handcuffs on you and shove a gun into the middle of your back." Malcolm laughed big and jolly-like.

He covered his eyes with one of his large hands and replied, "Oh, Elizabeth! When are you going to learn that I'm always going to beat y—" Elizabeth jumped down from the rafters, leaving the ropes behind to knock out Malcolm's henchmen. She quickly took their weapons, handcuffed Malcolm, and shoved a gun into the middle of his back.

"You were saying, your Majesty?" asked Elizabeth, wiping the blood from her nose with her blue t-shirt and reached around to take the cell phone from his jacket pocket.

"That took me eight seconds by the way," said Elizabeth, gloating as she began dialing. Her partner picked up his phone on the first ring.

"Agent Ward."

"Louis, I need three units sent to the old Winchester warehouse. The smuggled artifacts are in the south basement and a few of Malcolm's henchmen are knocked out in the east back room."

"How did you know where you were?!" asked Malcolm, angrily trying to turn around.

"Your henchmen talk a lot when you're not around, your Majesty. Now shut up and start walking."

"ELIZABETH! Are you alright? I've been so worried! Everyone was!" exclaimed Louis.

"Right, sure they were. That's why Madam Helen called off the search two weeks ago, right?"

"How did you know about that? I swear, Elizabeth, I wanted to keep looking but she said you were missing far too long and that you were dead because there was no trail to follow!"

"Malcolm's henchmen are gossiping old women. How else do you think I found out? How could I leave a trail? I had no freaking clue where I was until I got back to London. What happened in Paris, Louis? Why were you not at the café?"

"Excuse me, but you're using up all of my monthly minutes. I went over last month, and I can't go over this month again or they'll double my bill!" whined Malcolm.

"Where you're going, you don't need to worry about your monthly phone bill. Never mind, I can hear the sirens, Louis. But this conversation is not over!" Click. Getting to the door, Elizabeth kicked it open and was greeted by sunlight so bright, she had to shield her eyes with one hand. The wailing sirens and squeaky car brakes came to a halt in front of the warehouse door. Agents scrambled from the vehicles and ran over to Elizabeth.

"Get him out of here," said Elizabeth, shoving Malcolm over to three agents. Malcolm turned around to get one last look of Elizabeth before he was dragged away.

"Be seeing you around, darling," Malcolm said, winking at Elizabeth.

"Yeah, in court!" she shouted before almost falling over from the huge bear hug her stepsister Karen gave her. Wincing from the pain in her ribs but trying not to show it, Elizabeth hugged Karen back.

"Elizabeth! I was so worried about you! Are you okay? Oh, my goodness, look at your face! Those creeps sure decorated it," exclaimed Karen with her thick British accent, pulling back from the embrace and handing Elizabeth a black hooded sweatshirt and a pair of shades to put on that another agent brought her. It was freezing still at the eight AM hour, so Elizabeth tugged on the sweatshirt and put on the shades before speaking to her stepsister.

"Did you find the artifacts?" Elizabeth asked in her American accent.

"A unit is packing them up to take back to the correct museums as we speak."

"Good. You five," said Elizabeth, pointing to a group of agents beside her and Karen. "There are three men still in the back room that need to be brought to headquarters for questioning."

"Yes, Ma'am!" They shouted and ran into the warehouse. Turning back to her stepsister, the pause she used to take a breath caused Elizabeth to wince again.

"I need to find my jacket," said Elizabeth, starting for the warehouse, but Karen caught her arm and held her back.

"Hey, Harvey! Go in and find Elizabeth's black moto jacket please. It's freezing out here!" Karen told an agent, who in turn sprinted back into the warehouse.

"Thanks . . . Ahem. How mad is she?" Elizabeth asked Karen.

"Maybe you should ask her yourself," replied Karen, pointing to yet another vehicle with sirens wailing pulling up right in front of the ladies. An agent in the passenger seat got out and opened the door behind his. Out of the vehicle stepped a strong built woman in her late fifties wearing a bulletproof vest. Standing in front of the ladies, she put her sunglasses on top of her head and with a sigh crossed her arms.

"You sure made a mess out of Paris, Agent Cameron."

"Ma'am?" Elizabeth replied as she hung her head and looked down at her boots before looking back at the intense stare she was getting from the Director.

"MI6 tore the city apart with the assistance of Paris authorities, figuratively speaking of course, looking for you. And what do we find? Absolutely nothing because we had nothing to go on! You've been an agent for how long?"

"Since I was sixteen, ma'am."

"So, you graduated four years early from the academy. And you're twenty-three now?"

"Yes ma'am," said Elizabeth, ducking her head again.

"And you couldn't leave us some kind of clue as to who took you or where they took you?" The silence stretched on for what seemed like hours. Shaking her head, Madam Helen spoke again.

"I'm incredibly disappointed in you, but because you're MI6's best agent, I will look past this little screw up of yours. Do not let it happen again. Is that understood?"

"Yes ma'am," Elizabeth muttered.

"Good." Turning to the two agents behind her, she said to them, "A moment gentlemen, if you please." As soon as the agents turned their backs, she grabbed Elizabeth and hugged her hard. Again, Elizabeth winced in pain and tried not to show it.

"I'm so glad you are okay! I was so worried about you!" whispered Madam Helen in Elizabeth's ear, who was Karen's mother and Elizabeth's adopted mother. Pulling away and standing up straight again, Madam Helen said, "Supper is at seven sharp, ladies."

"Yes, ma'am!" exclaimed Elizabeth as Karen simply nodded.

"Perfect. Then we can discuss your next assignment," said Madam Helen, tapping an agent on the shoulder, signaling for him to open the car door so she could leave.

"Might I ask, ma'am, what the assignment is?"

Madam Helen smiled, put on her shades and got into the car. Rolling down the window she answered, "Why, babysitting of course. Back to AXL, Mitch." The car sped off, leaving Elizabeth and Karen exchanging looks of confusion.

CHAPTER THREE: THE ASSIGNMENT

"Could you pass the mashed potatoes please, Elizabeth?" asked Madam Helen.

"Yes, Ma'am," replied Elizabeth, picking up the bowl of potatoes and passing them to her adopted mother. Helen, Elizabeth, and Karen were sitting in the dining room eating a supper of mashed potatoes, peas, baked chicken, Caesar salad, and chocolate cake. Before leaving the room Jameson, Helen's butler, poured Helen a glass of Merlot and Karen a glass of Chardonnay. He did not offer Elizabeth any wine because he knew she did not drink before she had to leave for an assignment.

"That will be all, Jameson," said Helen.

"Yes, mum." Jameson replied, placing the bottle of Merlot next to Helen and quickly left the room. Helen turned to her adopted daughter as Elizabeth finished up her supper and moved onto her huge piece of chocolate cake. Karen reached for her piece of cake, but Helen took the plate from her hand and placed it out of her reach.

"It's not good for your figure, dear. I don't understand why Mary Ellen brought out a piece for you. You cannot eat desserts like Elizabeth. You'll be as fat as your grandmother was." Not as stunned as one would think she would be after a slam like that, Karen just reached for her wine and took a sip.

"Lizzy, you're such a great agent! I'm so proud of you for putting Malcolm away once and for all!" beamed Helen, reaching over to squeeze her adopted daughter's hand while Karen got a hurt look in her eyes and looked down at her lap. Taking her hand away from Helen, Elizabeth turned the attention to another subject matter that needed tending; trying to get the hurt look out of Karen's eyes. She hated seeing her sister hurt, especially by her own mother.

"So, this new assignment is babysitting?" asked Elizabeth, taking a sip of water. This question made Karen raise her head and look at Elizabeth with a small smile.

"Right, your next assignment, of course, I almost forgot. Have you heard of the UK pop superstar sensation Justin Max?" asked Helen.

"Justin Max? I love him! I have, like, all his albums! I have his autograph and a t-shirt with his face on it . . ." rambled Karen, until she saw the disapproving look from her mother and closed her mouth.

"Yes, I think I've heard something through the grapevine about him," answered Elizabeth very calmly; even though in truth she had his three albums, but unlike her sister she'd gone to most of his concerts during his last UK tour six months ago. He was a great musician, and rather not bad to look at.

"Is there a threat on his life or something?" asked Karen, putting her elbows on the table and leaned in to hear more about her favorite superstar.

"As a matter of fact, there is, Karen. Mr. Max has been receiving death threats from someone called 'Your Favorite Stalker'."

"How original," mumbled Elizabeth as Madam Helen continued.

"These threats have been received via email, text message, phone call, and snail mail."

"That's regular mail, mom," Karen pointed out.

"Right, yes, of course it is. Anyways, the recent threats have been the worst. 'The Stalker' is counting down the days until they arrive at Mr. Max's house to meet him for the first time. We have stationed agents at his home. Since his uncle is the prime minister, naturally he called us and asked us to protect his nephew. That's where you come in, Elizabeth. You take him to a secure location and lie low until the perpetrator is caught, or until you catch him yourself, whichever one comes first," finished Helen, leaning back in her chair.

"When do I start?" asked Elizabeth.

"You start tonight. Finish your cake quickly; you'll most likely have a few long weeks ahead of you, my dear, and you must report to me every two days."

"I'll be on my way," said Elizabeth, taking a sip of water and standing to give her adopted mom a kiss on the forehead.

Before slipping on her shades, she walked toward the front hall and turned back before she opened the front door as Helen called, "Good-bye my dear and good luck!"

Elizabeth waved back and replied, "Bye! Be good, Karen!" Karen winked but turned back to her mother before she heard the front door slam behind Elizabeth.

"May I be excused, mom? I'm meeting Jim at nine and we're going dancing at Tape London," said Karen, beaming just mentioning her boyfriend of one year.

"Yes dear, you may, but before you go out with that boyfriend of yours, I will remind you that I do not approve of that lawyer. Also, you need to finish that spreadsheet for my morning meeting tomorrow," replied Helen, getting up from the table and immediately, Jameson walked in with the head housekeeper Miss Kate in tow to clean the table.

"Jameson, I will be working in my study late tonight. Around nine could you bring me a glass of Scotch on the rocks? And please remind Mary Anne that if she wishes to remain in my employment, Karen will never have a dessert served to her again," says Helen as she headed to her study around the corner from the dining room.

"Certainly mum!" Jameson called after her, while he and Miss Kate continued to clean the table.

As he took an armful of dishes to the kitchen, Miss Kate turned to Karen, who was still sitting at the table and whispered, "Miss, would ye like me to bring ye a piece of that cake in a bit while you finish that work for ye mother?" Karen's eyes lit up.

"Please!" said Karen, getting up from the table and started to leave the room. "Miss Kate?" Miss Kate stopped piling up the plates to turn around and face Karen.

"Yes miss?"

"I have to make a business call for work, so could you bring it up in half an hour?"

"Yes miss," said Miss Kate with a curtsy. Karen frowned at the maid.

"We discussed that, did we not?" asked Karen.

"Yes miss. Sorry miss," apologized Miss Kate, looking rather sheepish.

"It's alright. You do not need to curtsy to me when mom's not around," she said with a smile and turned around to go to her room.

"Yes miss," answered Miss Kate, turning around to finish clearing the table as Jameson walked back into the dining room. Karen got to the huge winding staircase and suddenly stopped to gaze at its beauty. *This all will be mine very soon.* She thought and began to climb the stairs. At the top of the staircase, she quickly went into her room that was just off to the left. Walking to the huge walk-in closet, she opened her sock drawer and hurriedly threw the entire drawer contents of socks on the floor. Pulling a key from the pocket of her jeans, she unlocked the bottom of the drawer. Putting the key back into her pocket, she opened the false bottom of the drawer and pulled out a disposable cell phone she'd bought earlier that morning. Before dialing, she crossed to her bedroom door to shut and lock all three of her locks. Returning to the closet, she flipped on the light switch before she went in and shut the double doors. Karen dialed the only number in the phone's directory.

"Hello?" answered a voice.

"She took the bait," said Karen. "Elizabeth is on her way to that bloke's flat right now as we speak."

"Excellent. You've done well, Karen. Dispose of this phone and I'll contact you in three days for an update."

"Affirmative," said Karen and ended the call. *Now to dispose of this phone before my mother finds it and finish that spread sheet. Oh, and to eat that piece of cake! I hope Miss Kate brings me a big piece!* She thought, as she opened the doors to her closet and walked into the main part of her room.

CHAPTER FOUR:
THE SPEEDY GETAWAY

Parking her red mustang in front of Justin Max's mansion, Elizabeth got out and took off her shades for a moment. *This guy makes what I make in a year in less than two weeks!* She sighed, put her shades back on, and locked her mustang. Before she got to the front door, she was confronted by two other MI6 agents.

"Halt! Who goes there?" asked the tall agent who pointed his gun in Elizabeth's direction.

"Stand down, Frank and Pete. It's me, Elizabeth," she said, holding out her badge to show them.

"Oh! Agent Cameron! We do apologize, but we had to make sure you were not the 'Stalker,'" said Frank, after he and Pete put their guns down.

"I understand. But what's with the 'halt?' Why don't you try something else like, 'State your business,' or even, 'Hey, what do you want?!'" said Elizabeth, crossing her arms.

"Yes ma'am!" The agents replied. Neither of the agents moved to let Elizabeth ring the doorbell.

"Move it!" shouted Elizabeth, which made the agents jump. They moved out of her way and Elizabeth gave them a smile before she rang the doorbell. A man in his late sixties answered the door. Elizabeth pulled out her badge before speaking.

"Agent Cameron, MI6," she said, putting her badge back in her jacket pocket.

"You're a Miss? I do beg your pardon, ma'am, but I was expecting a male agent. Aren't all agent's male?" asked the butler.

"Yeah, I get that a lot and no, not all agents are male."

"Right. I'm terribly sorry, Agent Cameron. Come in, come in! Mr. Justin is almost packed!" said the butler, opening the door wider and ushering Elizabeth in. She stepped inside the mansion and the butler closed the door.

"Thank you," she said once she was inside.

"Please wait here, Agent Cameron, I will go inform Mr. Justin of your arrival," said the butler, who hurried up the staircase that lay in front of them. This left Elizabeth to gawk at the unique antiques that were in the room. Painted vases, a throne, and many portraits that covered the walls. She was looking at a painted picture of what must have been the superstar's family, when bounding down the stairs came Justin Max himself, speaking in a thick British accent. *American accents are no fun. I wish I had a British accent,* she thought.

"Sorry to keep you waiting, Agent Cameron, I was just finishing pa . . ." he stopped mid-sentence and in mid-bound because Elizabeth turned around still wearing her shades. Putting her shades on her head, Elizabeth pulled out her badge again and briefly showed it to him before putting it back in her jacket.

"I'm Agent Cameron, MI6," said Elizabeth. Justin was staring at her, but for what reason Elizabeth had no clue. She had blonde hair that was a bit below shoulder length and a bit too wavy for her own taste, hence the always in a ponytail. Blue eyes that she thought looked gray, physically fit although she thought she needed to lose at least twenty-five pounds but couldn't give up cake or ice cream and was about five-nine or five-ten the last time she bothered to check. By no means was she as beautiful as her stepsister, so Elizabeth assumed that she had something on her face, or he was just really surprised that she was female. Justin, on the other hand, was even more handsome than he had been in any concert she had seen him in. He had shaggy dirty blonde hair, long enough but short enough at the same time. This man definitely worked out; he was not too bulky, but his muscles showed through that tight black t-shirt of his. And his eyes . . . but she had to snap out of it. She could not even remotely think about Justin Max as anything but her charge. Besides, she remembered very clearly about the last time she had been involved with a charge. Finally, both Elizabeth and Justin snapped out of it before things got too awkward. Justin finished descending the staircase quickly and reached out to shake Elizabeth's hand.

"It's a pleasure to meet you, although I thought you would be a male agent," said Justin, holding onto Elizabeth's hand for a little too long. *Knew it,* she thought as she pulled it out of his grasp.

"I get that a lot. Can we get going?" asked Elizabeth, knowing that this job was going to be strange.

"George!" Justin called over his shoulder. George, the butler, came to the top of the stairs with a pillow in his hand.

"You shouted, Mr. Justin?"

"Can you bring my things down so that Agent Cameron and I can get going?"

"Certainly sir. I will be back post-haste!" replied George, turning around and hurrying to gather Justin's things. While awkward introductions happened in the mansion, a black ford pickup came pulling up the driveway. Frank spoke into his walkie-talkie.

"Frank to Neil, Frank to Neil, there's a black ford on premises. Repeat, there's a black ford on the premises, over." Static followed. Frank spoke again.

"Neil, do you read me? Over." Again, static followed.

"Hey! I know that truck! That's something Malcolm would

use!" exclaimed Pete, reaching in his pocket to dig his cell phone out to call Elizabeth, while Frank held his gun at the ready. Inside, Justin and Elizabeth had Justin's things and were just about ready to head back to the front door when Elizabeth's phone started to ring, playing one of Justin's hit songs. Blushing, she pulled her phone from the back pocket of her jeans, and she was surprised that Pete's name showed up on the screen. *Couldn't he just knock on the door?* she thought.

"Pete?" answered Elizabeth, confused. The connection was a little fuzzy because he had her on speaker.

"Code word Duke. I repeat code word . . ." Pete cut off abruptly.

"Damn!" cursed Elizabeth, shoving her phone inside her jacket while she rushed to the door to look out the peep hole. Getting there, she vaguely saw the truck park. Realizing that it was Malcolm's men who drove the truck and seeing the two thugs that got out of the truck take out Pete and Frank, she locked the door and looked around the room. Quickly sliding a table in front of the door, she turned to Justin and muttered, "That should buy us a little time." She pulled out her gun and took the safety off before she placed it back in the holster attached to her jeans. Elizabeth turned and started running up the stairs, only to pause halfway and look down at Justin still standing in the middle of the front room.

"Are you coming?" she yelled, already annoyed by a man who probably thought too much of himself.

"What's going on?" he asked as he walked to the stairs.

"Do you have a faster speed than half?" Elizabeth shouted, turning to finish sprinting up the stairs. Justin jogged up the stairs and found Elizabeth rushing around to different rooms. Trying to find a secure hiding spot for Justin, she bumped into his butler carrying a handful of sheets.

"I say, Mr. Justin! What on earth is going on?" George said, clumsily dropping the sheets and putting his hands on his hips.

"I haven't the foggiest, George. Agent Cameron has yet to fill me in," Justin replied, leaning up against a wall with his arms crossed and a grim expression on his face.

"Agent Cameron, could you please tell us what is going on here?" asked Justin. Getting to a room that had a balcony, Elizabeth rushed over to the open doors and looked over the railing. George and Justin entered the room behind her. Rushing past the butler and his master, she began yanking the sheets off the bed and started tying them together.

"Now see here, Madam! I just made that bed, and I will not have you messing it up!" exclaimed George, rushing over to stand next to Elizabeth with hands on his hips; outraged at the manner this woman was destroying his nicely made bed.

"In about a minute, it's not going to matter if this bed is made or not," said Elizabeth, dragging the four bed sheets that she tied together over to the railing of the balcony. She tied one end to the railing and threw the rest of the sheets over the railing to the ground. Elizabeth turned to her now two charges, wondering who volunteered her services for this assignment in the first place. Oh, right. Her mother.

"If you want to live, you had better start climbing down right now because in about thirty-six seconds two highly trained killers are going to come up those stairs . . . and probably kill us all." Immediately, Justin went over to the balcony, climbed over the railing, and started to the pavement below. The butler, on the other hand, had not moved an inch. Elizabeth glared at him and pointed to the balcony, but he shook his head.

"Madam, I refuse! I will not be leaving this house!" he said.

"Fine! I do not have time to argue with you," said Elizabeth, closing the doors to the balcony. Going over to the open bedroom door, she shut it just enough so she could see out a sliver.

"Three, two, one . . ." BOOM! Elizabeth heard the front door being broken in. The butler jumped at the sound. Rushing over to the balcony doors and flinging them open, he about jumped over the railing! Grabbing the sheets, he started down to the spot where Justin was waiting. Elizabeth just shook her head and turned back to the noise coming from downstairs. A moment later, she knew that the two men had started climbing the stairs. *Good thing I most often carry a spare grenade,* she thought, pulling it from her pocket and continued listening for steps coming up the staircase. By the sound of them, it was Scar and Rock, Malcolm's top goons, and Elizabeth knew at that moment that it could be the end of her as she knew it. Since the room was at the end of the hallway, Elizabeth watched quietly while they checked all the other rooms. When they had four rooms to go before hers, she quickly opened the door and opened fire while pulling the cord from the grenade with her teeth. She threw it toward the goons and . . . Ka-BOOM! The blast sent Elizabeth sprawling across the room as she was shutting the bedroom door. She hit her head on the wall on the other side of the room and winced in pain. Scar stumbled into the room. Elizabeth jumped up and prepared for the fight that was going to happen. Scar ran at Elizabeth swinging his fists. She ducked and swung her leg out to knock him on his backside. Scar jumped out of the way and grabbed Elizabeth's neck with his very large hand. Being the tall man that he was, he lifted Elizabeth into the air and flung her against the wall, sore rib side first. Elizabeth held her side and tried to shake it off, but the pain was very overwhelming and really getting to her. Having her back to Scar, she did not see him come up behind her and grab her by the neck again and yank her up. She tried prying his hand away, but he held on tight. Rock came limping into the room and stood beside Scar.

"What shall we do with her now?" he asked, sitting on the bed.

"Kill her like Malcolm ordered," replied Scar, squeezing Elizabeth's neck more. She squirmed in his grasp.

"But he never said how we had to do it," Scar said grinning as Elizabeth struggled for air to breathe.

"I say we just shoot her and be done with it. I'm tired of chasing her," said Rock, trying to move what looked to Elizabeth like a broken leg. She carefully took one hand and reached for her gun. Scar and Rock weren't the brightest bulbs in the pack, but it was getting harder and harder to breathe so this needed to end quickly.

"Hey . . . guys," Elizabeth gasped, "How . . . about . . . we . . . end this . . . now!" Grasping her gun, she pulled it out and shot Scar in the kneecap causing him to drop her. Elizabeth kicked the injured kneecap and then tripped Scar and he fell on his backside. Kicking him in the face for good measure left him unconscious. Elizabeth turned and pointed her gun at Rock.

"Hey now, I didn't mean to do it! He made me!" Rock said with his hands up.

"Tattling? Really, I thought you were too old for that," she said walking closer to Rock and holding her injured side at the same time. Holding the gun to his head she asked, politely of course, "Do I even have to ask who sent you?"

"You know who sent us! He just misses you is all, and he wants to see how you are doing," he said with a smirk.

"Tell Malcolm he is going to get what's coming to him," she replied before smacking him across the head with her gun knocking him out. Putting her gun back into the holster on her jeans, she hurried to the balcony and looked down. Justin was standing, waiting for her with his arms crossed, but the butler was nowhere to be found. She swung her leg over the railing and climbed down.

"What took you so long? And why is your head bleeding?" Justin asked when she landed on the ground. Reaching a hand up to examine her skull, sure enough, her head was bleeding.

Wiping her hand on her jeans and tightening her ponytail, she asked, "Never mind that, where's your butler?"

"George went home," Justin replied, and Elizabeth shook her head.

"Let's get out of here before Rock and Scar come to," she said, turning to run to her mustang. Justin caught up to her just as she opened the driver side door.

"Where are we going? And whose Rock and Scar?" asked Justin.

"I'll explain on the way." Climbing into her Mustang, she put on her seat belt and started the car.

"Are we going to the hospital? You really should get your head checked out," said Justin, getting in the car and putting on his seat belt. Elizabeth laughed at what she thought was a joke but stopped when she saw the serious look on his face. *Not a joking man. Got it.*

"No, we have to get you someplace safe. Your 'Stalker' is still out there," she said, reaching into the back seat and finding a black baseball cap, Elizabeth tugged her messy ponytail through the hole in the back of the cap and pulled the cap down over her bleeding head.

"Who were those guys?"

"They're just after me; don't worry about it. What kind of music do you like?" asked Elizabeth, looking through her CDs.

"Uh, doesn't matter," said Justin, looking rather uncomfortable.

"Good," said Elizabeth, putting in her party mix. Speeding out of the driveway, Elizabeth rolled the windows down and cranked up *Fancy* by Iggy Azalea just as Rock and Scar came stumbling out of the front door.

CHAPTER FIVE: ADIEU

Meanwhile, during the ruckus at Justin Max's residence, Karen completed her mother's spreadsheet, consumed a huge piece of chocolate cake, put on her favorite little black dress to go dancing with her boyfriend and she was already late. Grabbing her six-inch, neon-orange sparkle heels, her purse, and keys, she quickly raced down the staircase and out the door to her car.

Twenty-ish minutes later at the Tape London . . .

Showing her ID to the bouncer, Karen stylishly flounced into the club. Spotting Jim at the bar, she walked over to him and wrapped her arms around him.

"Hi there," said Karen, kissing Jim long and slow. Jim pushed Karen away and took a sip of his drink.

"What's wrong? I know I'm a late, but my mother made me finish her spreadsheet for tomorrow's meeting and Elizabeth got home tonight . . ."

"Enough Karen, I'm so sick of your excuses," Jim interrupted, finishing his drink and signaling the bartender to bring him another.

"They're not excuses Jim; I had to finish that spreadsheet for the Sawyer meeting tomorrow but whatever. Do you want to dance, or do you want to . . ." Karen smiled and leaned in toward Jim again, only to get pushed away. Again.

"I want a girl who is here. On time. Thanks Joe," Jim answered and then thanked the bartender who brought him another beer.

"What? What do you mean?" asked Karen, wobbling on her heels and sinking into a bar stool next to Jim.

"You heard me. I can't sit around forever waiting for you. I've been waiting for you in this club for two hours . . ."

"I told you I had to finish some work and Elizabeth . . ." interrupted Karen, reaching over to touch Jim's hand who snatched it away quicker than Karen had time to react.

"Are . . . are y . . . are you . . . are you b . . . breaking up with m . . . me?" stuttered Karen, suddenly feeling lightheaded.

"Yes. Yes, I am," replied Jim, as a tall, flaming red haired beauty swept across the room and encircled her arms around Jim's waist. After planting a long kiss on his lips that made Karen feel like gagging, she turned and looked at Karen.

"Is this her, babe?" she asked Jim, with her thick accent. Karen thought it could have been Australian.

"Sadly, yes. This is her," answered Jim, who stood up from the bar stool to wrap one arm around the woman's waist. Karen just stared at the woman in front of her who clearly was more beautiful than she was. Then she finally found her voice.

"Who is she?" Karen exclaimed, having an idea who she was but not wanting her suspicions to be confirmed.

"Oh, I'm sorry! You two have not been properly introduced. Stacy, this is Karen, my ex-girlfriend I have been telling you about. Karen, this is Stacy. How do I explain Stacy? Well, you should have found out sooner or later, but being the dumb brunette that you are, you never could put two and two together. Stacy is the woman that I have been seeing behind your back for the past eight months. Sorry to break it to you this way, but you don't deserve me. You never have. I deserve someone who is never late. Stacy is the woman you will never be. So, in closing my little break-up speech, I bid you a . . . how do you say it, babe?" asked Jim, turning to Stacy.

"Adieu, darling," Stacy replied before Jim kissed her passionately.

"Thank you. I bid you adieu. Have a nice life, or whatever. Let's dance, Stacy," said Jim, turning and taking both of Stacy's hands and starting to lead her to the dance floor.

Stacy turned back in Karen's direction only to say, "It was nice to meet you, Karen! Bye!" After watching them disappear into the crowd, Karen turned back to the bar, tears rolling down her cheeks. Joe, the bartender walked over to Karen.

"Rough night, huh?" Karen looked up and then reached into her handbag for a handkerchief and began to dab at her eyes. Nodding, Karen looked at Joe.

"You have no idea," answered Karen, finishing wiping her tears away. Putting her handkerchief back in her handbag, she asked Joe, "Would you mind getting me a double of whatever is the strongest drink you have?"

"Coming right up!" A few minutes later, Joe brought back blue liquid in two shot glasses. "Here you go! And the drinks are on me tonight," Joe said with a wink as Karen gulped down both shots with barely a breath in between. *Not bad. The shots or the man.*

"Just for the record, that guys an idiot. You're smoking hot and if I had you, I would never let you go," Karen smiled as Joe continued, "I'm actually getting off now. Can I buy you another drink?" he asked, leaning over the counter. Karen didn't think twice and leaned in to kiss him on the mouth.

Breaking away, Karen leaned in further to whisper in his ear, "How about we just go back to your place?" She pulled back to plant another kiss on him. This time, it was more passionate.

"Give me two seconds," said Joe, and he practically sprinted to the back of the club. Karen giggled. *Take that Jim. I can get any guy I want. I just hope Joe won't be brokenhearted when I don't call him tomorrow*, she thought as Joe arrived behind Karen's bar stool.

"My lady," he said as Karen slipped off the stool and took Joe's offered arm.

Handing Joe her keys she said, "You can drive my car," as they walk out of the club, with the music of Jesse James's *Wanted* following them out into the cool night air.

CHAPTER SIX:
IT WAS THE SECRETARY, IN THE OFFICE, WITH THE LETTER OPENER

Helen was talking, or rather yelling, on the phone when Elizabeth walked silently into the room. Helen frowned and motioned for her to close the door. Unknown to Helen, Elizabeth locked the door behind her.

"Call you back Debra. I said I'd call you back!" yelled Helen as she slammed down the phone. Crossing her arms and leaning back in her giant red office desk chair, she glared at Elizabeth.

"What, on the Golden Book of MI6, are you doing here? Where is your charge?" Elizabeth didn't reply and quicker than a blink, she snatched the letter opener off the desk and plunged it into Helen's neck. Helen's hand flew to her neck, startled eyes widened in surprise and hurriedly tried to reach for the phone, but Elizabeth got there first. She yanked the telephone cord from the wall and put her hands on her hips to smirk at Helen; taunting her, practically begging her to try again to call for help. Helen pushed the silent security button underneath her desk and received a laugh from her adopted daughter.

"Nice try mom, but I disconnected that weeks ago. There's no escape," said Elizabeth, zip tying Helen to her big red office chair. Surprisingly, Helen had not muttered a word since the stabbing, but Elizabeth wasn't taking any chances, so she found the duct tape in the top right-hand drawer and tore a piece off to fit Helen's mouth. Stepping back, Elizabeth paused a moment to admire her handy work. The blood seeped from the Director's neck, where the letter opener was still in place; nice and snug. Looking at the Director, Elizabeth carefully peeled off her face.

Helen got a wild look of horror in her eyes as Karen grinned back at her.

"Hello, Mother. What? No response? Oh, that's right, your mouth is taped shut! Get it? Taped-shut? Fine, don't laugh, it wasn't that funny anyways. I'll cut to the chase because I know how you HATE to be kept waiting." Karen smiled evilly before she continued, "I hate you. You always put Elizabeth before me; up high on a shelf like some prized trophy just because she's an agent and I'm not. In fact, I'm nothing, I'm just your secretary. Well, guess what MUM? I'm taking over. In fact, I'm taking over London. I'll be the best Director of MI6 by letting crime bosses and their henchmen run free all over the city. Oh, don't worry, you can watch from up there . . . or down there? Either way, you can watch from the sidelines." Karen glanced at the clock behind the desk on the wall, "Oh my! Look at the time! Time for Elizabeth to blow up the building and Karen to come back from break and put on the water works; she's SO good at that." Karen put back on the Elizabeth face once more and looked at her mother, who had tears running down her face.

"Don't cry. Your precious Elizabeth will be taken good care of. I'll make sure of it. She'll be very comfortable in prison, unless I decide to kill her myself, then you'll see her very soon!" Walking to the door, Karen turned to face Helen one last time.

"You know, I really do love you, Mummy dear. Truly. Even if you never cared for me at all; when I was your own flesh and blood to begin with." Karen opened the door and left the room as she shut the door behind her. She stood tall and walked out the front doors of MI6. Walking over to her red Mustang, she got in and closed the door behind her. Taking a deep breath, she looked at her keys. The red panic button stared back at her. If she went through with this, if she did what she set out to do, do more than she was ordered to do, she would press the panic button and that would trigger the bomb that was in the ceiling above Helen's head. She glanced at the button again, closed her eyes and pressed it. The building in front of her stood unchanged. Karen frantically pressed the panic button again and again. Whipping out her smart phone, she checked the camera she had placed in Helen's office a month ago. Helen was still in the chair, gasping for breath. *Tsk, Tsk. This won't do at all,* thought Karen, quickly dialing the number of the phone that she placed in her mother's desk; that was also a trigger for the bomb. BOOM! Smoke and flames started coming out of Helen's fifth floor office window. Karen smiled to herself, *Plan B always works.* Rolling down all of her windows as fire trucks and police cruisers whipped into the parking lot of the supposed White and Brown, Attorneys at Law Office, Karen turned on her radio and cranked it when she heard it was playing *Imma Be* by the Black-Eyed Peas. "Elizabeth" raced off to her car crushing appointment because Karen had to get back to the scene of the crime and be the lawyers frantically crying secretary, a part she knew she could play well. *Just wait till my sister finds out that Mummy dearest was murdered . . .*

CHAPTER SEVEN:
WANTED: DEAD OR ALIVE

"Are we there yet?" asked Justin, glancing over at Elizabeth impatiently.

"No," replied Elizabeth, rolling up the windows of her mustang. *Why is it that when I have a mission, it's always raining and cold?* she thought, turning the heat up in the car.

"Are we there yet?" Elizabeth took a deep breath before she answered.

"No."

"Are we there yet?" Her hands gripped the steering wheel before she answered him again.

"No."

"Are we there yet?" She pressed her lips into a tight line before she answered him yet again.

"NO."

"Are we there yet?!" Justin asked, throwing up his hands.

"I swear, if you ask me that question one more time, I'll make you sleep for the rest of the trip!" she shouted, gripping the steering wheel even harder in order to not reach over and smack her charge upside the head.

"Someone gets aggravated easily!"

"Only when you're involved."

"I say, will you at least tell me if we are in London anymore?"

"Honey, we haven't been in London for a couple days now."

"Are you kidding me?! We're not supposed to leave London!" Justin glared at her, outraged.

"Says the guitar-less musician to the agent with the gun.

We're going where I say we're going. If you want to stay alive, you need to do EXACTLY what I say," Justin rolled his eyes and looked out the passenger side window. Several peaceful minutes went by without any conversation. She glanced over at her charge. If he acted a little mature, she might be attracted to him. She shook her head. Don't even get her started on his eyes . . . *Ugh, snap out of it! He's just a charge, nothing more! You cannot go down this road again! You're a professional! Act like one! You can be this close to a hot man without wondering what he would look like with his shirt off . . . Oh, Come on! Look where you ended up last time! Miami! And LA, New York, and Vancouver . . . Not that it wasn't nice while it lasted . . . Stop it! Focus on the mission! The company wasn't bad last time, but obviously the company this time is better . . . CAMERON! JUST DRIVE!* Elizabeth thought, gripping the steering wheel even tighter. Just then, her phone lit up with Karen's name on it playing David Guetta's *Work Hard, Play Hard*.

Karen? She never calls me in the field. Something's wrong.

"I love this song!" exclaimed Justin, turning to look at Elizabeth. *Keep it together. Just pick up the phone.*

"Agent Cameron."

"Where. Are. You."

"On location. You know I can't tell you that."

"Well, you better stay off the grid or you will end up just like Mum!" Karen exclaimed through the phone, starting to sob. Elizabeth felt like she couldn't breathe, trying to process what Karen had just said.

"Where's the Director?" Elizabeth asked. Karen continued to sob.

"Karen, you need to stop crying and tell me exactly what is going on. That's an order."

"No one orders me around, least of all you!" Karen muttered into the phone.

"What? Karen, you must speak up. I cannot hear a word you're saying."

"I said, brace yourself, it might be more than you can bare." Elizabeth shuttered, not knowing what to think.

"Karen, just spit it out!" Elizabeth yelled into the phone, causing Justin to jump.

"Mum is dead!" Elizabeth stared straight ahead as if in a trance. Tears blurred her vision and the hand that was on the wheel slid off onto the seat beside her.

"Agent Cameron? Are you quite well?" asked Justin, glancing over from the passenger seat as the car swerved into the oncoming traffic lane. Justin reached over and yanked the wheel to slide the car back into safe driving grounds.

"You could have killed us! What is the matter with you?!" yelled Justin, loud enough to pull Elizabeth from her trance. She quickly blinked back her tears and grabbed her earpiece from the cup holder and fitted it on her ear. She placed her phone in the cup holder and placed both hands on the wheel.

"Right. Sorry about that. I've got it now. Remove your hands from the wheel."

"Are you sure? That was pretty much . . ." started Justin.

"I said I've got it!" yelled Elizabeth. Justin took his hands off the wheel and just stared at her.

"Fine," he said as he turned his attention back to the passenger side window. Elizabeth shook her head.

"Karen, you need to tell me what happened."

"Was that Justin? Can I talk to him please? You know I'm such a huge fan . . ."

"Karen, I need you to focus right now. Where is the Director?" A huge pause happened before Karen answered. "Karen?"

"In a body bag. Well, parts of her at least." Elizabeth didn't seem to notice that Karen had stopped crying.

"Parts? Explain. Now." Karen sighed. Elizabeth didn't seem to register that it was a sigh of annoyance.

"Think about it, Elizabeth. Her office blew up. I'm surprised that there were even pieces to find! There was nothing left but pieces. Except..."

"Except, what? Karen, what aren't you telling me?" The pause that followed this time just made Elizabeth angry. "KAREN!"

"Agents found your DNA..."

"Karen, I'm in her office all the time for debriefings and conferences and assignments..."

"...On the murder weapon," Elizabeth fell silent, "Elizabeth? I tried to explain that you're her *adoptive* daughter and you're out on assignment, but Bruce wants your head on a platter. He has sent out an alert to all agencies in Europe and Asia and even the CIA in the United States, telling them that you are to be shot on sight. No exceptions. You have been flagged. I'm sorry, Elizabeth. I did everything I could."

"I'm not surprised. He would be the first to... wait, Bruce? Why..."

"He's Assistant Director and temporary Director till I get trained in." Elizabeth couldn't believe her ears.

"You? But you're not even an agent!" yelled Elizabeth.

"Yes me, Elizabeth. I'm her bloody related daughter after all. But never mind that. What are you going to do?" Elizabeth tried not to let on how much those words stung, especially coming from Karen.

"I'll call you when I'm safe."

"But Elizabeth..."

"Karen, listen to me. Do nothing to make them suspect that you have spoken to me. Deny that you called me if they find out. Next time, I'll call you. I'll fix everything."

"Oh, I bet you will," muttered Karen.

"What was that?" asked Elizabeth.

"I said stay safe, sister."

"10-4," said Elizabeth. She rolled down her window and picked up her phone. She put her knees up to the wheel and started driving with them.

"What in the world are you doing?!" yelled Justin, reaching over to take the wheel again. Before he even got close, Elizabeth pulled out her gun and pointed it at him. Justin pulled his hands back quickly. Elizabeth put her gun away, took apart her phone piece by piece and threw every piece out the window, including her ear piece.

"Give me your phone," she said, holding her hand out to Justin. He said nothing as he handed over the smartphone that he retrieved from his jeans pocket. Elizabeth took his phone apart as well and threw it out the window as she took the wheel with her right hand and pulled a U-turn into the oncoming traffic lane and began to head back the way they had been coming from.

"Where are we going now?" asked Justin, who had crossed his arms and seemed to be angry with Elizabeth for destroying his phone. Elizabeth smirked and stepped on the gas pedal.

"To see a friend."

"Where's this friend?" Justin asked. Elizabeth just sighed.

"Listen. We are probably going to be spending a lot of time together for the next few weeks, so you are going to have to trust my judgment, alright?"

"Okay. But you are going to have to start telling me what the heck is going on!"

"How about I tell you what you need to know when you need to know it? That sounds fair to me." Justin just shook his head.

"Fine. Can you at least tell me where we are going?"

"London, because that's the last place they would look for us; in plain sight."

"Wait a minute! Us? What are you talking about?"

"Need to know information. You do not need to know yet, so sit back, relax, and enjoy some Matchbox 20." Justin groaned as Elizabeth rolled down the windows and cranked, *She's So Mean* while they made their way back; not knowing that a jet plane from Vancouver had just landed on a small airstrip just outside the busy city of London. A face from her past was on board and knew naught if they were intending on destroying her future.

CHAPTER EIGHT: ED THE SHOEMAKER

"Do I have to wear this ridiculous looking jacket? It has Winnie the Pooh on it! And it's very large on me!" Justin whined, pulling the jacket away from his body to prove his point.

"Stop complaining, " said Elizabeth, adjusting her black head scarf and sunglasses as they walked down the sidewalk in Soho, which is an area of the City of Westminster, part of the West End of London. "Besides, do you really want your fans to recognize you right now? 'Oh, Justin! Marry me! Oh, Justin! Sign my shoe!'" Justin raised his eyebrows as Elizabeth continued, "And then MI6 would find us before you could sing, 'O, Christmas Tree.'"

"But it's June…" he started.

"Then pretend it's snowing!" she replied angrily, trying to pick up the speed a little bit but changed her mind when Justin lagged.

"But it's still June…."

"Oh. My. Gosh! You are so . . ." she paused, looking for the precise words she would use to describe Justin Max.

"Ridiculously charming?" he offered.

"Nope," she said and blushed.

"Ridiculously good looking?" he said, as he grinned and winked at Elizabeth.

"Definitely not," she replied, rolling her eyes at him.

"How about ruggedly handsome?"

"I was going to go with super annoying . . ." she started, but quickly grabbed his hand as they walked past a couple police officers.

"Officers," Justin said as the police officers tipped their hats. She pinched the inside of his hand as her mouth formed into a frown. Justin flinched at the pinch.

"We're a couple that's in love, just out for an afternoon stroll to the shoe store; not speaking to the authorities." He shook his head and took his hand from hers and draped it across her shoulders. Elizabeth took a deep breath and laced her fingers through the hand that he had across her shoulders. Justin smiled.

"Excellent idea, darling. I do need a new pair of trainers." He leaned over and kissed her cheek as she smiled back.

"Just one thing: tell me why we're running from the law, again?" he whispered into her ear as they turned the corner to start down the street of their destination. She sighed before responding.

"If, I tell you, will you stop asking me?" she whispered, just loud enough for only Justin to hear.

"That's very possible, darling," he said in a normal tone of voice. She glared at him as he returned a smile.

"MI6 want me dead or my head on a wall; whichever comes first," she whispered. Justin shot her a confused glance.

"But aren't you one of them? The good guys, I mean?"

"Yes, but I think I'm the only good guy right now, so you're going to have to trust me, okay?" She turned to look at him, almost the way she would have shot her sister a look when they were growing up when Karen tried to sneak out and Elizabeth caught her.

"Alright. Will you at least tell me where we're going?"

"Don't you remember, silly? You need new shoes, and Spectacular Shoes has the best of everything," she replied, nodding her head toward the shop that was still a few businesses down the street.

"We're running for our lives, and you actually want to go

shoe shopping?! Typical woman," he muttered. Elizabeth laughed and shook her head.

"You have a very cute laugh," Justin said seriously.

"Really? I've always hated my laugh. My adopted sister used to tease me about it when we were growing up . . . I, uh, just have to pick up a few things. And you need to let me do all the talking; so please keep your mouth shut. Got it?" *What are you doing, Elizabeth? He's a charge, why are you sharing so much personal information with him? Keep it professional,* she thought, as she detached herself from her "boyfriend" and opened the door to Spectacular Shoes for a customer that was leaving.

"Thank you! Come a . . ." the tall, muscular, and bald shop owner started to say until Elizabeth walked in and took off her sunglasses and scarf, shaking out her wavy blonde hair. His eyes got wide as Elizabeth dropped the head scarf on the floor and shook out her hair again before putting her sunglasses on her head.

"Eddie!" she said, smiling as she walked toward him.

"No! No! No! No!" the shop owner shouted as he walked past Elizabeth and locked the front door and flipped the *Open* sign to *Closed*. He pulled all of the blinds down on the door and two front shop windows before he turned to face Elizabeth with his arms crossed.

"Eddie . . ." Elizabeth said again, putting her hands on her hips.

"I want no part of whatever you've gotten yourself into this time! I am not hiding you from anyone ever again!" he exclaimed, using his hands to make ridiculously looking hand signals at Elizabeth.

"Not me, him," she said, jerking her thumb back toward Justin, who had his arms crossed and was leaning against the door frame.

"What?" Justin said, as if coming out of a trance.

"Him? What did he do?" Ed asked, looking a bit confused.

"Long story short, he has a stalker. MI6 is after me, so he's not safe anywhere near me. Can you hide him? Please?" she asked.

"Alright, fine. I'll hide him but consider this a favor and you owe me big time."

"Deal," Elizabeth answered, trying unsuccessfully to cover her smirk.

"Now then, are you in need of any of your toys? I made some minor modifications; I hope you don't mind." Ed crossed his arms as Elizabeth's eyes lit up at the slightest mention of her toys.

"Never do, Ed. Can I see them? Please?" she pleaded.

"Hit the lights will ya, sonny boy?" Ed directed toward Justin, still leaning on the door frame.

"Don't call me that," Justin replied, flipping off the lights.

"Touché," Ed muttered to Elizabeth as he walked past her in the dark. She rolled her eyes and followed Ed over to the counter by memory. Hearing Ed press a button, Elizabeth held her breath as lights came up on the counter. Pressing two more buttons, the counter flipped over to reveal a handful of weapons that the royal military branch had not been given access to yet. Actually, no one had been given access to them yet because they had just been invented. Ed or Eddie (as Elizabeth liked to call him), short for Edward, was an inventor of advanced weaponry for Elizabeth Cameron only.

"Are these even legal?" Justin asked, walking up to the counter to gaze at the weapons that sat upon it. Elizabeth glanced at Ed before she responded.

"Who wants to know?" she asked, picking up a semi-automatic pistol.

"My prime minister uncle wanted me to be a military man. I learned about the advances they are working on for the crown in the academy before I dropped out to pursue my passion: music. I love to sing and hated the academy. From what I learned in the academy, it doesn't take much to determine that this is new weaponry. I've never seen anything like this before . . ." he started, taking the pistol from Elizabeth's hands. She hadn't pegged Justin to know anything about weapons, much less to have studied at the military academy. Not with that gorgeous head of hair and those beautiful eyes that when the light hit them just right seemed to shine brighter than the moon. Justin looked up as Elizabeth stared at him. Blushing furiously, she turned her attention back to the other weapons on the counter, which were mostly guns and some knives as well.

"As a matter of fact, young man, I . . ." Ed started to tell Justin that he, himself, had created the weapons he saw before him, but Elizabeth shot him a look that shut him up.

"Where's Bug? I only count fifteen. Where's my Bug?" Elizabeth asked Ed, worriedly glancing through the rest of the weapons.

"What's a Bug?" Justin asked, putting the pistol back on the counter.

"Ahh, the watch. I had to completely remake that piece since you destroyed him in Paris!" replied Ed, angrily crossing his arms.

"Hey now! Don't get all defensive! I was ambushed!" Elizabeth shot back, leaning on the counter.

"What happened in Paris?" Justin asked no one in particular, as he moved closer to Elizabeth. In that very instant, Elizabeth felt the butterflies in her stomach that should not have been there. *No. This CANNOT happen again! Remember what happened last time you fell for a charge? Lock up your heart. You cannot have another incomplete mission. Your life and everyone's you care about depends on it.*

"Nothing, just complications," she muttered as she placed both hands on the counter and started an intense stare down with Ed. Within a few minutes, Elizabeth won.

"I shouldn't even let you have him," Ed said, turning behind him to take a photograph of a collage of shoes off the wall to reveal a safe behind it. Punching in the combination, he reached in to produce a watch that he gingerly passed to Elizabeth, who slapped it onto her wrist, at the grimace of the shoemaker. Ed placed a pair of black boots onto the counter and Elizabeth gave him a smile before she took them. Justin found it odd that the pair of boots that she wore and the pair that Ed had given her were very similar in design, but he said not a word as Elizabeth switched the worn and dirty pair for the clean pair. Ed came around the counter to stand beside her as she finished putting on her new boots.

"What's the mission this time?" Ed asked her. Returning to a standing position from her kneeling position that she had been in to change her boots, she looked at Ed and shook her head.

"You should know by now I can't tell you that. I wouldn't even if I could, I don't want to put you in danger," she said, turning to look at the weapons line-up to determine what she should take with her.

"But you have nothing to lose now," Ed said, and Elizabeth froze.

"What did you say?" she asked him, turning back to stare up at him directly in the eyes.

"What I meant was that since your mum was murdered . . ." Ed started, seemingly not wanting to back down from another stare down with Elizabeth that he knew he was going to lose.

"What?" Justin interrupted. He had been silently leaning against the counter, watching the Ed and Elizabeth show and saying naught a word. Elizabeth blushed again, knowing Justin's eyes were on her, and dared not make eye contact because she did not know what would happen after that.

"This was neither the time nor the place to bring that up!" she told Ed angrily.

"Agent Cameron, is that what the phone call in the car was about? Why did you not tell me?" Justin asked, as he placed a hand on her shoulder. Elizabeth felt like she couldn't breathe as time seemed to stop. She suddenly wanted to forget everything and lean into Justin and . . . *Oh, be still my beating heart . . . wait, what?* Taking a deep breath, she shook his hand off and placed a small blade into her left boot.

"Agent Cameron, answer me," Justin said as Elizabeth placed another blade up her left jacket sleeve as Justin came closer to her still. *Focus,* she thought, as she unzipped her jacket and put a side arm into her other gun holster. Putting her dried, bloody hair into a ponytail and zipping her jacket back up, Elizabeth grabbed the automatic pistol and walked to the front door and unlocked it. In a last-minute decision that her head told her was a horribly bad one, she turned back to the man that she thought she was falling for, having a sudden need to tell him everything.

"I didn't tell you that my mother was murdered because it was need to know information and you didn't need to know. Now that you know, you may as well know that MI6 has flagged me and wants me dead or alive because they think I murdered her when I was off babysitting you. In Paris, I was kidnapped by the crime boss of London, whom another agent and I had been sent to capture. I'm going to go see what dear old MI6 is up to and contact my sister. Stay here and out of sight. Ed, if I'm not back in two hours, activate Plan 16."

"What's Plan 16?" asked Justin, taking a step toward her.

"Ed will let you know if the time comes to it," Elizabeth glanced down at the pistol in her hand and then tossed it back to Justin.

"Just in case," she said, turning and opening the door to be greeted by the setting of the sun and evening shoppers. She didn't hear Justin call, "Be careful," as she shut the door behind her. Putting her sunglasses on, she headed off to MI6 headquarters, not knowing that what she would soon discover would most likely tear her apart.

CHAPTER NINE: RIGHT UNDER MY NOSE

Karen drummed her fingers on the tabletop in the coffee café. Louis was late. *Why is he always late?* she thought as Louis burst into the café out of breath.

"Dearest Karen, please forgive me for being late, I ran into traffic," huffed Louis, coming over to her table and trying to kiss her. Karen just held up her hand.

"Sit, dummy."

"Quite right. My apologizes," Louis said, as he moved to sit across from her. There was only one other customer in the entire café. Louis wondered why Karen had picked a place with so little business and why she hadn't ordered them both coffee and perhaps even a sandwich. He was starving because he hadn't eaten lunch and it was too close to supper to eat anything but a meal.

"Shall I get us some lattes and maybe a tuna sandwich?" he asked her, but quickly realized that he would not be eating anytime soon. His stomach grumbled in response to that.

"Why haven't they found her yet?" asked Karen, ignoring his question.

"Found whom, my darling?" he asked, leaning toward Karen with his elbows on the table.

"Are you serious? Elizabeth, you idiot!" Karen whipped out her phone and dialed the number of the person she wished to reach out of memory, completely ignoring Louis's wimp puppy look. *Maybe he's hungry. Maybe I should throw him a bone.*

"Hello, my dear. What can I do for you?" asked an older male voice on the second ring.

"Have you found her yet?" Karen said, raising her voice loud enough to have employees glance her way with an annoyed expression.

"My henchmen are at her condo on that private island offshore of Bali, but so far she is nowhere to be found."

"How could she not be there?! She wasn't at her summer home in Greece, she's not in Sydney or Cairo, so where is she?! How could we not have found her? Unless . . ." said Karen, pausing as she started to think.

"Yes?" asked the man on the phone.

"Unless . . . she never left. Why that little . . . nice try, Elizabeth, I've got you now! Malcolm, you need to get your men back here ASAP. I'll explain when they get back here. I have a plan," she said as she ended the call and slipped the phone back into her pocket.

"Let's go, Louis," she said as she got up from the table. Louis left a ten-dollar tip on the table and gave the employees a wave before catching up to Karen as she got in her convertible.

"Where are we going, darling?" asked Louis, climbing into the passenger seat and buckling up.

"I'll send someone for your car later," Karen answered as she climbed in and started the car before putting her seatbelt on. "Elizabeth wanted us to think she had left London, when really, she has been here the entire time, right under my nose," Karen said as she pressed on the gas pedal and merged into traffic.

"But where are we going?" Louis asked yet again.

"To see a shoemaker about some weapons," she muttered, slipping on her shades and Louis turned up the volume on a popular pop song that was on the radio. He wondered if they were ever going to find Elizabeth, for she had pulled a disappearing act before and had been MIA off the grid. If they didn't find her soon, they never would. Elizabeth had enough contacts, he supposed, that would help her leave the country in a heartbeat and vanish forever. When she had been missing before, she had been missing for almost a year, if he remembered correctly. That was after she had been assigned to protect what's his name, when they were fresh out of the academy. That had been a mess in itself and look at how bloody well it had turned out in the end . . .

CHAPTER TEN:
SPYING ON THE HOME TEAM

Night had fallen. The temperature had turned very nippy, and Elizabeth shivered in her jacket. *Why do I never dress well enough for the weather?* she thought, hugging her jacket closer. She wore that jacket always, since her graduation from the academy. Helen had said that it had been her, well, Karen's grandmother's before she passed. Elizabeth felt privileged to wear the jacket, especially since Jennifer Austin had been said to have been a top MI6 agent in her younger days, before she disappeared in the field in her forty-fifth year. Elizabeth tried to remember pictures of Jennifer she had seen when she was a child as she stood on the rooftop across from the new MI6 office. *Where are all the guards?* Looking through Ed's binoculars that she had borrowed without permission before she left Spectacular Shoes, she turned up the volume on the binoculars, which doubled as a listening device. Ed believed it best to carry as little as possible when on a mission, so he often made two-in-ones. Elizabeth listened closely as the Assistant Director spoke on the phone.

"Yes. Yes, I'll see to it personally, Karen. I'm sending a team your way." *Karen's in on this? She can't be.* Elizabeth thought, as she watched the Assistant Director, Bruce Bingham, hang up his phone.

"Mark!" Bruce bellowed as he rushed to his open closet door to retrieve his bulletproof vest. Bruce finished strapping it on as a breathless agent, Mark Hibbins, hurried into the room.

"Yes, Assistant Director?" Mark said out of breath.

"Send out four teams to retrieve Elizabeth Cameron," Bruce said, dashing back to his desk to take his handgun from his top drawer.

"Four teams?! Five team members per team; twenty agents for a retrieval mission?!" Mark asked.

"Very good, Mark. Now I know you can do simple multiplication. SEND TWENTY AGENTS to go and retrieve Elizabeth Cameron and bring her to me!" Bruce barked, pushing past Mark out of the office as he headed to the elevator.

"Don't you mean to justice, sir? Or do you still have a thing for her?" teased Mark, as he stopped at his desk to grab his gun from his drawer and hurried to catch up with the Assistant Director. Bruce whirled around to face Mark; stopping so abruptly that Mark almost bumped into him.

"Of course not!" Bruce yelled as Mark crossed his arms and arched an eyebrow. Bruce sighed.

"Okay, fine, it's very possible that perhaps I do have a thing for Agent Cameron."

"Ha! I knew it! Sir, you've got to get over it. You know you have no chance with her," Mark exclaimed, jabbing a finger in Bruce's direction.

"We almost kissed! How could I forget about something like that?" *It was a holiday party, and you were drunk and tried to kiss me . . . before I broke your nose.* Elizabeth remembered, smirking at the thought of breaking that toad's nose in front of the whole agency.

"May I remind you, sir, that you're still at the office?" Straightening up, Bruce put on a stern facial expression.

"Let's go, Mark. Time to bring Elizabeth Cameron to justice for the murder of Helen Austin." *I didn't kill her!* Elizabeth fumed from her position.

"But sir?" Mark started, as they waited for the elevator.

"What is it now?" Bruce grumbled.

"You haven't told me where to send the teams."

"Didn't I?"

"Negative, sir."

"Hmm. Must have slipped my mind." *How you became Assistant Director, I'll never know, but I'm almost 99.5% sure you poisoned the previous Assistant Director. Without prints on the wine glass, I'll never prove it . . . legally.* Thought Elizabeth, shivering in the cold night air.

"Send them to Spectacular Shoes. It's in Soho. Some guy named Edward Carlson owns it. You can Map Quest it," said Bruce, heading into the elevator with Mark on his heels, already on the phone. "Tell them to be on their guard; for all we know, Elizabeth Cameron is watching us right now," said Bruce, lifting his head to look Elizabeth directly in the eye before the elevator doors closed.

"Mother of Pearl!" muttered Elizabeth, dropping the binoculars with a clatter and looking around for a quick exit as she pressed Bug's ON button.. *The only reason Bruce said what he said and then looked right at me, was that someone told him. He's too dumb to figure that out for himself. Who tipped him off? Are they watching me right now?* she wondered as she radioed Ed.

"Ed, do you copy?!"

"Loud and clear, Elizabeth," Ed said over the clear channel of the radio waves.

"I've been had! We've been had! I think Karen sold you out! They know I'm here! Get Justin out now! Activate Plan 16! Now!" she exclaimed and then she heard muffled sounds in the background.

"Someone's breaking in!" Ed whispered.

"Can you hold them off? I'm on my way! I'll be there in fifteen minutes! Tops!"

"We won't be able to . . ." A crash was heard through the radio as static followed.

"Ed? ED!" Elizabeth shouted into Bug as two agents burst

through the roof door.

"Great," Elizabeth muttered, putting her hands up.

"Don't move!" one agent shouted as both agents advanced, their guns trained directly on her.

"Is there a problem here boys?" she asked, taking a few steps backward to the roof ledge behind her.

"I said, DON'T MOVE!" the agent named Joe said.

"Come on, Joe. We attended the academy together. You know I would never hurt an innocent person without probable cause. And you," Elizabeth started, as she glanced at the other agent, "I don't know you. What's your name?" she asked him as she took another step and continued to move toward the roof ledge, having only a couple steps to separate her from a great fall.

"Larry," answered the other agent.

"Hello, Larry. I'm Elizabeth. Nice to meet you. You seem like an excellent agent," she said, taking another couple of steps to the edge of the roof. Her boot heels hit the edge as she continued to have a casual conversation with the agents that probably wanted her dead. *All in a day's work,* she thought.

"Why, thank you. It's nice to meet you as well. I've heard so much about you . . ." he started, lowering his gun.

"Larry! She's on the list!" Joe yelled.

"What list?" Elizabeth asked.

"The list of agents that need to be taken care of," Joe answered, continuing to advance toward Elizabeth.

"Never heard of that one," she said.

"Bruce put it in play a few hours ago," Larry clarified. Elizabeth glanced at Joe.

"Can he do that?"

"He's the stand in Director. I guess he can do what he wants," Joe answered, still at the ready to shoot Elizabeth if she tried any funny business. But sometimes 'Funny' was her middle name.

"Joe, do you really think I killed my own mother?" she asked him.

"I try not to judge and go by the book," his eyes selling the lie better than his words were.

"I helped revise *The Book*. Having a hit list is definitely not in the book!"

"Joe, not to interrupt, but I'm sure she didn't kill her own mother. She seems way too nice to do something as horrific as commit a murder." Joe turned his attention to Larry and glared at him.

"We have no say in this! We just have to do what we're told!" Joe told him angrily, waving his gun in the air, seemingly without a care.

"But if it's not right, why should we follow through?" Larry responded with a question. With the agents appearing to be involved in a battle of right and wrong, Elizabeth saw her chance and stepped backward onto the edge of the roof.

"Hey guys!" she called, pulling them from their argument. Elizabeth saluted the agents and back stepped off of the twelve-story building.

CHAPTER ELEVEN: NO DEAL

"Why is it always raining in this city?" Karen exclaimed, pressing the button to bring up the top of her convertible.

"Because it's June?" offered Louis.

"Bloody awful reason if you ask me," Karen responded as her phone started singing Justin Max's current number one hit song.

"This is your ringtone?" Louis asked as Karen dug her phone from her jeans pocket.

"What of it?" she responded, handing the ringing phone to Louis.

"What am I supposed to do with this?" he asked, just looking at it.

"Answer it!" Karen yelled as he did.

"Hello! Karen's future husband speaking. Who may I say is calling?"

"Lou!" Karen exclaimed, snatching the phone from his hand and by doing so, racked one of her fingernails across his cheek.

"Oy!" Louis yelled and put his hand upon his burning cheek. "You drew blood, woman! How dare you?!" he exclaimed, outraged as he brought his hand away from his face to show Karen a few droplets of blood that had been smeared on his hand.

"You'll get over it and still love me," Karen replied, rolling her eyes as she brought the phone to her ear. Louis grumbled something about women she didn't catch. *Men,* she thought.

"Director Karen."

"What a nice ring that title has. And it suits you, Director," a man's voice said.

"Thank you. I have always wanted this title since my mother . . ." she stopped abruptly when she mentioned her deceased mother.

"I'm very sorry for your loss, my dear. Your mother was an extraordinary creature; that is, when she wasn't getting in my way. It was such fun to outsmart her back in the day when she was just a field agent. Over the years, I always had to be three steps ahead of her. You know, she caught me twice more than Elizabeth has. She caught me a total of five times . . ."

"Enough with how much better my mother was than Elizabeth! Focus on the agent that is alive, not the former agent who is dead!" snapped Karen angrily.

"I apologize. We need to focus on the capture of Elizabeth. I just wanted to point out that it was a pity that Helen went the way she did. In cold blood, I mean." Karen paused for a brief second before uttering the words she had wanted to since she had completed the task.

"I had to take care of her," she muttered.

"What?"

"I did it."

"You're going to have to speak up my dear, I am still unable to hear you. Maybe it's the location . . ."

"I murdered my mother!" Karen shouted so loud Louis jumped in his seat beside her. A few good minutes passed before either person on the phone spoke their thoughts.

"Hello?! I just confessed to the murder of my mother, the murder of the MI6 Director, quite possibly the crime of the century, and you have nothing to say?!" whined Karen, clearly annoyed with the man on the phone.

"Karen, there could be bugs in the car! Keep it down! Do

you want Bruce to hear you? You'll be sitting behind bars before you can say, 'Elizabeth is your sister!'" Louis said and realized what he said about five seconds after he said it.

"Adopted sister. Get it straight," Karen said.

"If only you knew the real truth," muttered Louis, crossing his arms.

"What was that?" Karen asked.

"I said, pay attention to the road."

"Hello? Are you still there?" she asked the person on the phone.

"Indeed," he replied firmly.

"Well, do I have your full attention now, Malcom?"

"As a matter of fact, you do. The deal's off," he said.

"But you said if I delivered Elizabeth to you . . ."

"You broke the deal when you murdered your mother," Malcom snapped.

"She needed to be dealt with! She was snooping! Besides, she was never a part of our deal anyway! You just wanted Elizabeth!"

"Do I have Elizabeth in hand?"

"No, but . . ." Karen started.

"No, I do not. In, fact, you neglected to inform me that MI6 is proceeding to capture her right now," Malcom said, very strangely calm.

"But that's protocol and I'm the Director and I have to go by the book . . ."

"Elizabeth helped write the bloody book!" Malcom yelled.

"She helped revise it, actually. She's not smart enough to write a book like that!" Karen shot back.

"You underestimate her too often. And by the way, just to refresh your memory: you're not *the Director* yet, nor should you ever be, but we will give you one more chance. Call us when you have Elizabeth to hand over to us," Malcom said coldly before hanging up, leaving a stunned Karen listening to the sound of the dial tone buzzing in her ear.

CHAPTER TWELVE:
FAST AND FURIOUS

"Can this traffic get any slower?" Karen complained, tossing her cell phone into the backseat.

"What happened now?" asked Louis, with his hand on the scratch that Karen left on his face, although it had stopped bleeding.

"Nothing of your concern," replied Karen, slowing down and stopping for a red light. She was finally the first car at the intersection, and it took her almost a full minute to realize that her car was the only one around. They were currently in the middle of Soho where it was supposed to be busy all the time, even that late during the night as it were. Karen frantically looked around and unbuckled her seatbelt in the process. She put the convertible in park and Louis looked at her strangely.

"What's wrong this time?" he asked, still clearly very annoyed with his future wife.

"Something's not right," she answered, reaching under her seat to try and find the handgun she kept there. "Haven't you noticed there's no one around?! No people, no cars, and no street cop that stands on the corner of every intersection in Soho?" she exclaimed, furiously still searching for her gun. Suddenly, from around the corner and out of sight, came a huge old station wagon that slammed into the front of Karen's convertible head on.

The airbags deployed as Karen and Louis struggled against them to try and overcome the other driver. The other driver flew out of the station wagon and rushed to the driver's side door of the convertible. Shattering the window with a good swift kick, the unidentified driver wrapped their arms around Karen's upper body and dragged her from the car onto the street, while rain poured down on them. The stoplight changed from red to green as Louis yelled Karen's name repeatedly, continuing to struggle less against the weight of the airbag and more so with his own seatbelt that he just could not seem to unbuckle. Karen's eyes were squeezed tight shut, desperately trying to pry her attacker's hands from her throat, where they were choking the life out of her.

The attacker loosened their grip a tiny bit to whisper into her ear, "I do not know how you get the information you do; no one knew where I was, not even you. If you interfere again, I will end you. It'll be a pity to do so, but, because you're my sister, I'll make an exception. And you have really awful taste in men," Karen's eyelids opened abruptly as she made out the form of Elizabeth driving away in the station wagon as rapidly as she appeared, while Karen gasped for air. She still lay in the street getting even more drenched for the raindrops had started to fall harder. The green light had changed back to red as Karen propped herself up on her elbows. Louis finally won the seatbelt battle that had turned into a war and stumbled out of the car to hurry over to a still gasping-for-breath Karen. Dropping to his knees beside her in a rain puddle, he stared at her for several long seconds before he uttered any words.

"Darling, are you alright? What a brute he was! Let me help you stand," he said, reaching down to take her hands. Karen shook him off and shakily stood up.

"Let's go," she said, opening the driver's side door and getting in. Louis raced to the passenger side and climbed in just as Karen put the vehicle in drive. Stepping on the gas, she ran the red light.

"Can you slow down please? You just experienced a trauma,

and we could get pulled over for the speed you're going and the car looking like this," Louis said calmly, earning an, *are you serious?* look from Karen.

"Pull me over? Ha! That's a laugh. No one pulls over the MI6 Director if they know what's good for them."

"Director-in-training," Louis muttered.

"What was that?"

"Nothing."

"Fine, be that way!" she exclaimed.

"Fine!" he huffed.

"Fine!"

"Fine!" she yelled as silence echoed in the car as Karen made a right turn.

"Karen?" Louis said quietly, looking at his hands in his lap.

"What?" she asked, still a little upset that Elizabeth had kicked her butt, but she was not about to let Louis know that her attacker had been a woman; her adopted sister as it had in fact been.

"Where are we going again?" Karen sighed before she answered him.

"We're going to see a shoemaker about some weapons."

"A shoemaker that makes weapons?" he said almost to himself, very puzzled.

"Particularly a BUG," clarified Karen, making another right turn, pulling onto the street of their destination.

"Does he know where that kid is?" Louis asked, seeing the flashing lights up ahead.

"Yes, yes he does. Now darling, if you would be so kind as to shut your trap, I must see to my first operation as the MI6 Director," she said, pulling up beside the curb, shutting off the engine quickly as she got out of the vehicle.

"Are you coming? Karen asked, not bothering to shut her

door and quickly walked up to Bruce as he stood in front of a shop called Spectacular Shoes. Louis stared after her. Man, this woman was confusing, but he loved the heck out of her. He knew they often didn't see eye to eye, but he knew that he was going to marry her in order to get a shot at the fortune.

 Climbing out of the car, he left the door open as he walked at a normal pace up to where Bruce and Karen were shouting at each other. He smiled and made a mental note to ask permission to marry her when this mission was all over, and it was the end of Elizabeth Cameron as they knew it.

CHAPTER THIRTEEN:
GREEN WITH GOLD SPECKS

After ditching the station wagon, Elizabeth carefully and skillfully crept along the rear side of shops in the village to get to Spectacular Shoes. It had stopped raining, the blood was gone from her hair, and her clothes were dry, but she hoped she had not ruined her jacket. Reaching the door of the shop, she realized with a strange fear settling in that she would not have to break down the door like she was hoping she would have to. She unzipped her jacket and pulled out a gun as she walked into the open doorway, careful not to trip the trick wire that Ed placed there to warn him of unwanted customers when they entered his shop. Stepping over broken glass, broken boards, and shoes that were scattered all over the shop, she reached down to pick up a lone Nike and in doing so, Elizabeth didn't have time to remove herself from harm's way. Seconds later, she felt the end of a shotgun pressing into the back of her skull.

"Any sudden movements and I'll blow your head off," said a voice that Elizabeth knew very well.

"Well, that's not very nice," she replied, slowing turning around to face a stunned Ed.

"Elizabeth! Thank goodness you're safe! We were so worried about you!" Ed exclaimed, hugging Elizabeth tight as he placed the shotgun onto the counter.

"We?" Elizabeth asked, pulling back from the embrace and looking at her longtime weaponry caretaker with confusion.

"Did I say we? What I meant was that, um, uh, the shoes and I are so happy that you're safe! Right guys?" he asked, turning to the shoes that were scattered about the tiny shop.

Elizabeth raised her eyebrow at the man that she had looked up to since the end of her academy days and whom she considered the father figure in her life. Gazing around the room, she tried to analyze the situation and shook her head.

"You need to get out more often, Ed." Elizabeth squatted down to grab a discarded bullet casing that did not belong to Ed's shotgun. Standing up, she handed it to Ed.

"They actually shot at you, huh? Was Justin hurt?" She waited patiently as Ed shifted his balance from one foot to the other and looked at her gravely.

"We were ambushed. They came at us from all sides. Although he fought well for a musician," he started, earning a slight smile from Elizabeth before Ed continued, "he unfortunately took a bullet to the chest." Elizabeth turned white as a sheet. She opened her mouth to say something but thought better of it as Ed continued his tale, "they dragged him away and someone hit me over the head with something," he finished, looking at Elizabeth for a reply.

"Was Karen with them?" was all she could muster for a reply, although she already knew the answer to the question.

"She oversaw the whole mess! What's going on, Elizabeth? What has she done?" he asked her.

"I don't have time to explain. What weapons were taken?"

"None of them. They didn't find any because they didn't search for any."

"They came just for Justin? There's more to this than meets the eye." Elizabeth started to pace as she continued, "They're bound to know now that you're my weapons supplier! Karen was the only one that could have known . . ." she said as she stopped pacing and started piling up shoes.

"Her and that side-kick of hers," Ed added.

"Yeah, well, Louis is attached to her hip, has been since the academy when he supposedly fell madly in love with her."

"Not that wimp, the other guy," Ed said. Elizabeth stopped her shoe sorting and looked at Ed again with confusion for the second time that night.

"What other guy?"

"Oh, you know, about six-one, excellent hair, tattoos on his forearms."

"What color were his eyes?" Elizabeth asked him seriously.

"Really? What color were his . . . Elizabeth, how in the world am I supposed to know . . ."

"What color!" she shouted at him. She blinked as he stepped back, stunned she yelled at him like that. She was surprised at herself; she had not expected Ed to bring up memories of love, hate, and betrayal. Composing herself, she readdressed Ed.

"What color were his eyes?" she asked him, quietly and calmly.

"A green with a glimmer of gold, I suppose. I don't know, I really didn't look that close."

"Green with gold specks," she said, grabbing another knife from the weapons collection that Ed brought up for her. She started for the back door as she heard Ed call out to her.

"Good thing, noticing details like that. Friend of yours?"

"He's my ex," Elizabeth replied, walking out the back door and disappearing into the night.

CHAPTER FOURTEEN: WHERE IN LONDON IS JUSTIN MAX?

Elizabeth took several deep breaths as she walked behind the shops, plotting her next move. Could he really be here? Hadn't she left him on that Vancouver Street corner in the pouring rain with a warning to never contact her again? She closed her eyes and for a moment she remembered exactly what she had said to her old charge, her ex-fiancé . . .

Vancouver, Canada, five years ago.

Putting her hands on her hips, Elizabeth stared him down. Tossing her soaking wet hair from the Vancouver rain over her shoulder, she took a deep breath before answering him.

"This? This is over."

"Don't be like that, babe. It was just one night . . . okay, maybe two . . . ah, who am I fooling? It was two months before you caught on!"

"And framing me for murder? What was that, just a formality?"

"That was an accident. That Matt chap was just in the wrong place at the wrong time."

"So, turn yourself in."

"Absolutely not! What would my mates say? 'Josh Hemingway is nothing but a softie' is what they would say! I definitely could not face them again if I turned myself in for a crime I didn't mean to commit!"

"But what about me?"

"What about you? I thought we were talking about my 'accidentally' murdering the agent."

"Now we're talking about us. What do you think that would

mean to me if you turned yourself in?"

"Um, let me think. You would gravel at my feet for me to take you back when I'm found not guilty and then we would live happily ever after? How close am I? Right on the money?"

"There you go again with the money! Do you care about anything else in this world?!"

"Actually, no. I really don't think I care about anything else but money. What else could I possibly need?" Elizabeth's breath caught in her throat, realizing what she was going to do.

"Josh, you better listen very carefully to what I'm going to say. This? This is over. I trusted you with my heart and you threw it back bloodied and bruised. So, Mr. Money, we're through. Do not contact me ever again. And don't even think about randomly showing up where I am, because I will take you out in a heartbeat and you know I can. MI6 will love me for that since they have been after you for quite a few years. I also returned the ring since it wasn't really mine to begin with," finished Elizabeth, as she opened the door to a waiting taxicab and left Josh standing on the curb in the pouring rain. *How am I going to explain this to Madam Helen?* she thought as she listened to the rain beat on the cab windows as it sped through the busy downtown streets of Vancouver, Canada . . .

Elizabeth opened her eyes. She knew what she had to do. She knew where Justin was. The trick, though, was to get in and find Justin and get out without drawing attention to themselves. She figured that it would be a quick and easy rescue mission until she figured out how to better handle Karen.

"But Josh is there," Elizabeth turned her head to the right and saw a miniature version of herself with a halo and wings and in a white dress that she would never be caught dead in. She fought the urge to laugh, fore when she turned to her left shoulder, there was another miniature version of herself with a pitchfork and horns in a red dress that she would never be caught dead in. The horned version of herself grinned at her and said, "It'll be quick and easy, and you'll get Josh back," Elizabeth gulped. Did she want him back? After all that he had done to her, all that he was. Did she still love him despite everything? Elizabeth pondered this as an argument started between the miniature Elizabeth's.

CHAPTER FIFTEEN:
ADVICE FROM ABOVE AND BELOW

"What in the world would make you think that she would want that good for nothing piece of . . . um, man back? Don't you remember what he did? I thought we discussed this recently," said Angel Elizabeth, putting her hands on her hips.

"You can't change the past, but Josh is back for a reason, and you remember that saying you loved as a child?" started Horned Elizabeth, "'If you love something, let it go. If it comes back, it's yours.' Perhaps this was meant for you and Josh. Maybe he's back for you. Deep down, you know you're still very much in love with Josh. You might as well be happy as you travel the world," Horned Elizabeth finished, bringing up Elizabeth's impromptu trip to New York, Miami, LA, and Canada.

"That was one time! I was young and naive and fresh off passing my agent exam! I had been drinking and that clogged my judgment a little bit," Elizabeth said, earning a glare from Angel Elizabeth.

"A little? Clogged your judgment a little?! Your judgment was clogged the minute he became your charge! You overlooked the fact that he kidnapped you and you jumped at the chance to travel the world with him! You barely knew him and went anyway! You accepted his proposal after only a few months of knowing him and took his word for whatever they were worth when he said he wasn't sleeping with Leslie or killed Matt! Hate to break it to you sweetheart, but he was sleeping with your cousin and then murdered her and murdered your childhood best friend. We both know you didn't know who he was until he murdered Matt; but honey, you stayed with him after you found out! Who does that?! I think I'll say what everyone else is thinking: Elizabeth Cameron, your head is not screwed on all the way when it comes to the notorious criminal Josh Hemingway. You SHOULD NOT go anywhere near him while he's in town!" Angel Elizabeth ended her long speech without really giving Elizabeth any suggestions, but silently giving her two options: she could either run, or she could face that man that she had thought loved her. The first man she had ever given her whole heart to, and he had broken it. She could run, but what about Justin? She pictured his gorgeous eyes all full of concern when she had told him about the demise of Madam Helen. She couldn't shake the feeling she got when she thought about him. She sighed. She was, unfortunately, quite smitten with her current charge. Maybe it's because he had been shot while in her care, or it could have been those eyes. Yes, it was those eyes. The eyes of a man had to give off a certain sparkle in order to captivate her attention. She glanced over at Horned Elizabeth, who had not uttered a single word in edgewise during Angel Elizabeth's entire speech. Horned Elizabeth was smiling at her.

"You're in love with Justin too, huh?"

"Me? Absolutely not!" Elizabeth said, blushing a deep shade of red.

"You're in love with two men!" she teased.

"Definitely not," Elizabeth said as she suddenly got an idea.

"Perfect!" grinned Horned Elizabeth.

"You cannot be serious! Are you out of what mind you have left? What kind of an idea is that?" asked Angel Elizabeth. Smiling, Elizabeth looked from one miniature Elizabeth to the other and uttered three words before they disappeared.

"Justice and Revenge."

CHAPTER SIXTEEN: BEHIND ENEMY LINES

This was suicide and she bloody well knew it. Elizabeth was standing in an underground hallway of the "new" MI6 headquarters. It had taken her ten minutes longer than she would have liked to get past the castle guards and forty minutes to get to the castle in the first place. The castle was on the outskirts of Surrey, and she was unsure of why this was picked for the new headquarters because she was pretty sure this castle was owned by Malcom Ferguson. Only a single torch lit the way down the dark, damp, and dreary hall. This was also about as creepy as getting lost in those catacombs in Egypt last July. The hallway smelt about the same: it smelt of death. She shuddered and silently crept along beside the wall, gun raised waiting for someone to jump out of the shadows. As Deja vu as it sounded, she felt she had been here before, in this very same castle. She couldn't put her finger on it, but she had been here before; perhaps she had been here searching for Malcolm once, but it made no difference. As if by memory she made her way to the dungeon, thinking that was where they would keep Justin, and finding the door unlocked, she raised her gun higher and pushed open the door. Her breath caught in her throat as a burning torch showed that in the center of the room sat a black eyed, tied to a chair, hunched over, dry bloodied mouth Justin. The room was empty, save for Justin and the pitter patter of tiny feet, which she assumed were rats. *Good thing it wasn't rats she was afraid of.* Putting her gun in the back waistband of her jeans, Elizabeth hurried over to one of her current love interests and started to try and untie the rope that securely held his wrists to the chair. She thought Justin was dozing and the moment she started working on the rope, Justin started yelling.

"DARLING! I KNEW YOU WOULD COME SAVE ME! Those awful brutes dragged me here to sit with the rats! Darling, do I look like a rat TO YOU?!"

"Shh! Do you want someone to hear you? We have to get out of here before they know you're gone, because when they do, they'll know I was here," she whispered, struggling with the ropes that held Justin fast, "Who tied these, a boy scout?" she muttered to herself.

"Some guy. I couldn't see his face and when I wouldn't tell them where you were, that WOMAN just would not stop hitting me!"

"Karen," Elizabeth muttered again.

"Yes, that's what the guy said when he pulled her away from me. Elizabeth, I have a serious question to ask you and I need you to give me a serious answer," Justin whispered. Elizabeth froze; her hands stopped their work on the complicated knots. She swallowed hard before she answered him.

"What?"

CHAPTER SEVENTEEN: SLIPPING UP

"Elizabeth, why is the sky blue?" Elizabeth started to panic when those words left Justin's lips. Forgetting about the knots for a moment, she went around and kneeled in front of Justin. Briefly touching his pale and cold face, she looked him worriedly in the eye.

"Justin, what did they give you?" He stared at her and started hysterically laughing. She tried to cover his mouth to stop the noise, but he bit her hand playfully and continued to laugh. She then placed both hands on his knees and Justin stopped laughing abruptly and gazed at her; a grin that went from ear to ear.

"You have such beautiful eyes. Did you know they shine in the light?" Elizabeth blushed and suddenly seemed to notice that he was bare chested without a shirt. Justin was trying and failing to lean toward her, probably because of his bound hands and wounded chest; she saw how he grimaced when he tried to get closer to her. Questions began to fill her head, and none of the questions were about what her next move would be; they all pertained to Justin. Did he want to kiss her? Should she kiss him? Did she want to kiss him? Boy, did she really want to! She quickly shook that thought from her head.

"Justin, what color was in the syringe? Did you see what color it was?"

"What's a syringe?" Elizabeth sighed. This was going nowhere, and they needed to get out of this creepy place.

"That thing that hurt you. Besides that woman?"

"Oh! That really hurt! It was red and that guy stuck it in so fast, I didn't know what had happened! Then I must have blacked out because the next thing I knew, you were breaking the door down to rescue me!"

"Well, that could be anything!" Elizabeth huffed, finally giving up on the knots and pulling a knife from her jacket sleeve and freeing Justin from his current predicament.

"I'm free!" he shouted and stood up, only to fall flat on his face. Elizabeth shook her head and smirked as he began to groan. She then grabbed his arm and forced him to stand, draping his arm around her shoulder as she hesitated only a moment and placed her arm around his bare torso. They had only taken two steps toward the door when Louis stopped them in their tracks.

"Elizabeth! I've been so worried about you! Is there something I can help you with?" he asked sarcastically. *Don't trust him!* screamed the voice in her head. She was unable to reach her gun and had to back step and help Justin back onto the chair. Grabbing her gun, she pointed it at Louis as he shot her in the left shoulder with his gun.

"Nice try," Louis said grinning. She blinked, realizing the bullet was a sleeping dart. She yanked it from her arm and willed herself to stay awake as her head began to feel heavy and her eyelids drooped. She dropped to the dungeon floor on her knees, but she forced her eyes open once more. As she lost her grip on the gun and it clattered to the floor, Louis caught her head and set it gently on the cold floor.

"He cannot wait to see you," Louis told her as Elizabeth drifted off into the second forced sleep she'd had in two months.

CHAPTER EIGHTEEN: FACE OF THE PAST

I must have slept on a rock, Elizabeth thought as she slowly opened her eyes. Trying to move, she found she had an extremely sore shoulder and was in about the same position she had found Justin in, tied to a chair. She had no weapons because they had relieved her of her jacket. That made her so annoyed, and she silently vowed that whoever possessed her jacket when she got out of here was going to get it. She was not in the dungeon either, she seemed to be in an interrogation room with just the door in front of her, another chair facing her, no windows, and a camera with the red record light blinking up on the ceiling to her right. The light above her was the only other thing in the room. She mentally kicked herself for getting caught. She shouldn't have gazed into those eyes of his. If she hadn't, she and Justin might have been in the clear.

Darn you, Louis! They probably moved Justin to another room, perhaps even another location! What was I thinking? That I could have kissed him? Get a grip! He's a pop star, I'm a secret agent. What am I expecting? A fairytale ending where Justin and I live happily ever after? I tried that already and where did that lead? I'm just like Karen. I really know how to pick 'em! Elizabeth sighed and concentrated on ridding herself of the ropes that held her hostage. What was this guy? A Navy Seal? Frustration set in as she began to figure out who had tied her to this chair. Then the door opened to reveal the subject of her thoughts, the person who she had loved and then lost. Horrible circumstances had brought that about. She frowned as he stepped into the room.

"Hello, love," he said, closing the door behind him.

CHAPTER NINETEEN: THE GAME OF TRUTH

"No hello? Not even for your ex-fiancé? That's cold, darling. We were together for a happy year before you ruined our little holiday."

"Seven months. We were together for seven months! And I didn't ruin anything! You did," Elizabeth yelled at Josh Hemingway. He frowned; a very deep frown that made him look like he had a unibrow. Josh moved to stand directly between Elizabeth and the chair she did not currently occupy. He reached out to cup her left cheek with his rough hand. She stiffened yet did not pull away. With Josh being this close to her again, after not seeing him for five years, Elizabeth knew a few things were most certain: she was most definitely still in love with him. Josh had been working out. Was it possible for him to have gotten even more handsome and even more, *gag*, irresistible than when he'd first been assigned as her charge? Perhaps, perhaps not, but none of it mattered because she was still going to kick his bum.

"That's no way to treat me, love, after all this time." That did it. She had been trying so hard to keep her cool, but that one word was about to make Elizabeth Cameron blow up like a volcano.

"You of all people in this big world, have no right, absolutely no right to call me that anymore!" she yelled at him. Still fidgeting with the ropes that bound her hands, she fumed. *If my hands were not imprisoned! Mother of Pearl! How dare he show up after all these years and expect everything to be just as it was?* Josh spun the chair opposite Elizabeth backward and sat on it facing her, sitting very improperly. It drove Elizabeth simply mad.

"Darling, could you please stop hurting your wrists? If you recollect, I was in the Royal Navy and that rope there is not coming undone anytime soon." Elizabeth sat perfectly still and stared at him, "There now. That's better, isn't it, darling? Now, I'm sure you have questions. Ask away, for I dare say we only have ten more minutes in each other's company."

"I only need five," she muttered, mostly to herself.

"Alright then, fire away," Josh said as Elizabeth took a deep breath before asking her first question.

"You stole the ring from Alexander's collection," she said, angrily glaring at him.

"That's not really a question, but yes, I did take that ring. You admired it so much, that I knew you had to have it. In fact, I took it back from his collection last month, if you would care to put it back on?" Josh reached into his suit jacket pocket and produced a small emerald bright green box. *Always overdressed in his black suit and tie. All he needs now is a top hat.* She thought as the box took her out of her trance. She would know that box anywhere. Her mouth went dry as she shook her head.

"Never," she said firmly as Josh sighed and returned the box to his jacket pocket.

"Next question," he said, looking hurt, but she ignored that look in his eyes. She'd seen it many times before; when he had lied to her time and time again, and he was not going to fool her twice.

"You murdered Leslie."

"Darling, I thought this was twenty questions, not the accuse Josh of everything he has supposedly done," she glared at him to continue, "Fine, fine, yes, yes, I did murder your cousin, but only because she had started to become extra baggage that I didn't feel like carrying around when you and I exchanged rings."

"And you were sleeping with her. You cheated on me because?"

"Ahh, a question I can answer. Well, to put it in the simplest terms you can understand, I was shagging your cousin because you weren't, oh what's the words I'm looking for? Oh, yes. Putting out," he grinned and showed her all of his pearly whites as Elizabeth blushed and frowned at the same time. She was becoming more furious after each answer. *Ignore that comment. Next question.*

"You murdered Matt."

"He was snooping around! What was I supposed to do when he showed up and wanted to take you away from me? I'm very sorry if he was your childhood best friend, soon to be partner in MI6 *and* madly in love with you, but I could not let the best thing that ever happened to me slip through my fingers," Elizabeth felt a slight feeling of love toward her ex-fiancé as he continued, "so he had to be dealt with," and the feeling was gone.

"And framing me for murder? What was that all about?"

"That, my dear, was just pure chance that the authorities found your prints on the murder weapon at the crime scene. Pure chance," Josh said.

"That has nothing to do with the fact that the victim was my cousin, and you told the police that I was jealous of the fact that you two were such good friends?" she shot at him.

"Absolutely not," he answered very calmly.

"I see," she said and frowned, not willing to meet his eyes.

"I do believe our five minutes are almost . . ."

"Last question," Elizabeth said interrupting. Looking at Josh directly in his eyes she thought for sure she had seen him cringe, and she loved that, "Tell me honestly, because I know you well enough to know when you're lying, so tell it to me straight. Were you ever in love with me, or was that just a game, as well?" With the long pause that followed and the examining of the shiny dress shoes of his, she had her answer, and the one, she silently admitted to herself that she was hoping for. Elizabeth swung her arms over her head and threw the ropes in Josh's face. She had the ropes already untied when they had begun that dreaded of dreaded conversations and she back flipped over Josh's chair, taking him with her. While she landed in a soft crouch, Josh's head hit the cement floor beside her. Elizabeth turned, stood up, and planted her boot on his throat. He gasped for breath as she stared down at him.

"I hope you have a concussion. That's the least you deserve. I told you not to contact me ever again. That basically means, if you didn't know, this conversation should never have happened, and you should not be on the floor with my boot at your throat, but it serves you right. Let me make myself very clear, because apparently, I wasn't clear the last time. Do not contact or come near me again, or I will end you," she paused, flipped off the camera and turned back to the man at her feet, "I'm going to find my jacket, and then I'm going to find Justin, who is, by the way, more of a man than you will ever be," she finished, pressing down hard on Josh's windpipe for good measure. She turned toward the door, the door that she'd never heard open, to find Karen grinning at her as the door shut behind her.

CHAPTER TWENTY: FACING THE DIRECTOR

"Hello, sister! Or, should I say, adoptive sister? Thought I would heed your warning, hmm? You should know by now that I don't ever follow orders, especially from you of all people." Karen crossed her arms and leaned against the door to clearly show there was no escape. Josh groaned from behind her, but Elizabeth paid him no mind and did not take her eyes off Karen.

"Karen, if you do not remove yourself from that door . . ." she started.

"You'll do what? Assist me in doing so?"

"I'll kill you," she finished. Karen looked at her and laughed.

"You don't know, do you? Ha! How could you know?"

"Karen, come off it and just tell her," Josh said from the floor. Elizabeth looked at the woman who had been one of her best friends for as long as she could remember with confusion.

"Karen?" she prompted. Karen straightened up and cleared her throat.

"It was the secretary, in the office, with the letter opener . . . and the bomb," she said with an emotionless face. Elizabeth was more than a little puzzled.

"Excuse me? Do you only speak in riddles now?"

"Give it a few minutes. It'll sink in," several minutes sped by all the while Elizabeth stood between her now ex-sister and ex-fiancé, looking rather dumbfounded. Karen began tapping her foot, signaling to Elizabeth that she was getting annoyed.

"Come on, Lizzy You used to love this game as a child!"

"Do not call me that."

"And why not?"

"Only mom called me that."

"My mom, Elizabeth," Karen spat, "Your mother gave you away. She left you. That must suck, knowing that no one ever wanted you in the first place? Time is running out for you, Elizabeth Cameron. Now name. That. Game." *Game?* she thought, as a little light bulb went off in her head.

"Clue," she answered, earning three slow claps from Karen.

"Wow. Give the girl a cookie, or how about a big piece of chocolate cake? You need to watch your figure, you're putting on the pounds." Elizabeth gave Karen another confused look and put her hands on her hips.

"Huh. I didn't think my bum was *that* huge. What do you think Josh?" she asked, glancing over her shoulder at where he had risen from the floor and slouched in the chair, she had previously occupied.

"Looks good from this point of view," he replied, giving her a thumbs-up. Elizabeth turned back to Karen and shrugged her shoulders.

"Your boyfriend says I'm good," Karen rolled her eyes and looked around Elizabeth to glare at Josh who grinned back.

"Whatever! Back to our little matter at hand. Why do you think I referenced *Clue*?"

"To play with my mind?" Elizabeth said, shrugging again.

"Come off it, Karen! Tell her you murdered your own mother!" Josh shouted. Elizabeth turned partway to look at him and she thought she saw sympathy in his eyes, but she did not look long enough to figure it out. Turning back to Karen, she found that she was grinning again. *She looks a little too comfortable leaning against the door like that.* Elizabeth thought, smiling back at her and opening her arms wide.

"Karen, I'm so proud of you! You had the courage to do away with Madam Helen when I couldn't! Let me give you a congratulatory hug!" Karen looked at Elizabeth unbelievingly.

"Really?" she asked, as Elizabeth crossed her arms.

"Yes, really! What do you think I'm standing here for, to show off my assets? Get over here, sis!" Elizabeth pulled Karen into a bear hug, much like the one Karen gave her after Elizabeth had been held captive by Malcom. Elizabeth pulled back from the embrace and smiled at Karen, and Karen returned that smile. Suddenly, Elizabeth jerked back and head-butted Karen, knocking her to the floor. She was out cold.

"Bravo, darling! Way to indicate whose boss! Jolly good show!" Elizabeth had almost forgotten her ex was in the room. Almost. Faking a smile, she went back to where he sat and socked him in the jaw. Finally satisfied, she quickly left the room, slamming the door behind her.

CHAPTER TWENTY-ONE: WORDS CAN HURT YOU

Elizabeth hurried down the corridor after finding her jacket that Louis was guarding, and it had felt good to be able to sock him in the jaw as well. As she dashed down the corridor, she felt lost. She'd been down one too many hallways and felt very small in this big castle. To make matters even worse, she had no idea where Justin was and an alarm had started going off a few minutes earlier, so she didn't have much time left before she was found. That sure put a damper on things. She quickly made another left and stopped dead in her tracks. Slowly she eased backward until she could see them, and they couldn't see her. Much to her dismay, Rock and Scar stood guarding a door at the end of the hall. *What're they doing here? Is Karen working with Malcom? No, she can't be because he's locked up . . . right?* She pressed a gentle hand to her rib cage. She winced. Her ribs were still tender. No way could she take them herself in the shape she was in . . . but maybe she didn't have to. She quickly unhooked Bug from her wrist; the only weapon that had not been taken from her during interrogation. Karen knew she had a weapon called Bug, but did not know what it looked like, probably why she hadn't confiscated a simple looking watch. She attached Bug to the castle wall, about ankle high from the floor and after pressing the "light" button, out shot a hook that embedded itself into the wall directly across from her. Peaking around the corner to make sure the goons weren't looking her way, Elizabeth carefully stepped over Bug and took a casual stroll about the hall. Partway down the lengthy hallway, Scar turned and stared at her. She stopped then and smiled. He elbowed Rock and the two goons started down the hall toward her.

"Well, look what we have here! A lost little girl! Do you need help finding your mother? We could help you with that," Scar said and then he and Rock laughed, an evil laugh that was heard over the blaring alarms that were still going off in the castle.

"I need some assistance today, sirs! Could one of you dummies point me in the direction that pop singer is being held captive?" Rock and Scar stopped mere feet away from her before Rock answered.

"Duh, he's in the highest room in the tallest tower. Why do you think we're guarding the door?" Scar hit him upside the head.

"You idiot!" he yelled as Elizabeth noticed a key ring hanging from Scar's front jeans pocket. Without hesitation, she stepped forward and snatched the key ring, which tore a hole in his jeans.

"Hey! After her!" Elizabeth started backing up as the goons advanced quickly.

"Karen's dead. I killed her," she fibbed. Rock and Scar exchanged looks but only shrugged their shoulders.

"So? That's a pity. Must have been awful killing your only living family members just days apart from each other. Malcom was saddened at the death of your mother. He told us himself."

"Malcom is in the Pentecost maximum security prison, where you two will join him shortly," Rock laughed as Scar grinned at her.

"Do you want to tell her or should I?" Rock said, smiling until a glare from Scar made him lose it.

"You should know by now that no jail cell will ever hold the

Crime Boss of London," she groaned at the words.

"He escaped?!"

"When most of the guards there are on his payroll, I think there is a fairly high chance of escape possibilities. If you recall, that's where you put him last time; whereas it took him three months to escape. It took him mere hours this time. On the other hand, it'll take the authorities decades to find your remains after Malcom gets through with you," Scar said. Elizabeth knew she had to make her move now, so she turned and ran for her Bug, keeping only just out of their grasp. She leapt over the wire as Rock and Scar tripped and fell smack on their heads. Scar must have hit his head really well because he was unconscious, but Rock on the other hand, held his bloody nose and was the perfect goon to grill for information. Elizabeth picked up Scar's gun that had skidded across the stone floor and kicked Rock's away from him. Kneeling next to Rock, she pressed the barrel of the gun to his temple. He whimpered as she spoke to him.

"Don't be such a baby!"

"I take after my mother . . . ." he whined.

"And I really don't care. Where's Malcom?"

"I know nothing!"

"You're saying it all wrong. Besides, this is present day, not an episode of *Hogan's Heroes*. Now tell me where Malcom is, and I just might not pull the trigger."

"I don't know where he is! Honest! All I know is that he is after you so he can put the Stalker game to rest because he grows tired of it," she froze at the mention of her current love interest's number one fan; besides her, of course.

"Does he know who the Stalker is?"

"Of course! He created him!"

"What are you getting at? That Malcom is the Stalker and

he sent me on a fake mission just to what, prove a point? That he's got me right where he wants me? Is that it?" Rock smiled up at her; a smile that made her cringe. All of a sudden, all of the alarms became silent, and she froze as Rock hissed a mere sentence that made her breath stop cold.

"Justin will be your undoing."

CHAPTER TWENTY-TWO: CONFESSIONS

Elizabeth stood up from her kneeling position beside Rock, grabbed Bug, and jogged down the corridor gripping the key ring so tight she thought she might draw blood from her hand. Putting the gun in the back waistband of her jeans, she fumbled with the keys. Most of them were newer looking and by the look of the lock on the door when she stopped in front of it, that lock hadn't been changed since the castle was built. She found an older looking rusty key and shoved it into the lock. Hearing the click, she pulled open the door and squinted into the darkness. Before her stood an ancient flight of stairs, which appeared to disappear above her head. *Great,* she thought. She shoved the key ring in her jacket pocket and began climbing them, quickly realizing that the stairs seemed to resemble the staircase that resided in Madam Helen's former home. She pushed back that thought from her mind so that she would not start crying. *There will be a time to grieve, but now is not the time,* she thought as she paused halfway up the flight of stairs to catch her breath.

"Lay off the cake, Cameron!" she muttered to herself, panting as she heard a very loud shuffle that echoed through the darkness. Someone else was on the stairs behind her; she could sense it. Refusing to panic, she climbed the rest of the stairs in a hurried fashion and found yet another door with a ray of light shining beneath it. *There're too many doors in this freaking maze!* Finding the door unlocked, she pushed it open to find nothing but a lamp burning and a still bare-chested wounded Justin; bound, gagged, and faintly breathing with his eyes closed.

Closing the distance between them, she was able to untie the ropes that bound his hands to the chair. Swinging Justin's arm over her shoulders she helped him stand as she placed her arm around his waist. Justin moaned as the other person stepped across the threshold into the highest room in the tallest tower where she, the knight, was rescuing the damsel, Justin. *How ironic,* she thought as the figure stepped into the light, panting harder than she had from climbing those stairs. Elizabeth glared at the man that she had put behind bars not once, but three times since she had become an MI6 agent, and every time she put him there, he managed to escape the clutches of a federal facility. Malcom Ferguson grinned at her.

"How is it that every time I seem to turn around, you're not where you're supposed to be?" he asked, crossing his arms over his big chest, still gasping for air.

"How is it that a man of your particular size, managed to climb a flight of stairs like that and not collapse?" she challenged, shifting her weight as Justin opened his eyes.

"Elizabeth?" he whispered, glancing from her to Malcom and back again.

"Elizabeth, I love you." Her heart felt like it had stopped beating in her chest as she wobbled in her boots. She tried to focus, but just couldn't get those words out of her head. *Maybe Rock was right. Maybe Justin will be my undoing. I must buy a little time and then I'll go willingly.* Hoping neither man would press her on the issue, she focused all her attention on Malcom, who interrupted her thoughts.

"I do not appreciate being the subject of fat jokes, Elizabeth; especially from you of all people! It hurts the most."

"You do have feelings. That's new," Elizabeth said, trying to determine how long she could push his buttons before he snapped.

"I certainly do! And I only care about me, myself, and I; and my own flesh and blood, but I do not take kindly to being insulted by my own offspring!" Elizabeth laughed out loud at the mention of offspring.

"That's funny, Malcom. Justin looks nothing like you," she said grinning, but her smile quickly vanished when she caught the smile from Malcom; a smile that made her blood run cold.

"Not that schmuck. You, Elizabeth, darling. You dear heart, a pain in my bum, are my flesh and blood," Malcom paused for the words to sink in for a dramatic effect and then continued, putting an emphasis on his next words, "You're my daughter, Elizabeth."

CHAPTER TWENTY-THREE: TO PULL THE TRIGGER OR JUMP

Elizabeth stared at Malcom. She barely heard Justin calling her name. She felt as if she were in a dream: a lovely dream that had her about to shoot and kill Malcom Ferguson, the criminal that always seemed to try her patience. She grabbed the gun from the back waist band of her jeans and pointed it straight at Malcom. She refused to let him break her.

"Nice try, your majesty. You've got to do better than that," she said, refusing to believe what he had said was true. She could do this; she could kill the King of London Crime. After all, he was London's current biggest problem. Who cared about justice? She would be a hero! She'd be hailed for ending Malcom's life, maybe even given a medal . . . but did she really want that? To be a hero? Play God, just like that, with Justin as her witness? She mentally shook her head to get rid of the thought. She faintly heard Justin saying her name. Seems he found his voice and not too soon. Elizabeth moved in front of the second man that had ever professed his love for her. *That subject will have to wait.* Malcom laughed at her. She would not miss that laugh nor would she miss that *"Jolly Holiday"* of a man.

"Now, now, darling, let's not rush to drastic measures. What would London ever be without the King of Crime?"

"A lot safer? Whatever game you're playing at, it's not going to work. In ten seconds, I'm going to blow your head off. One, two, three . . ." she started.

"Now Elizabeth, if you do this, you'll never know what really happened to your mother!" Malcom cautioned.

"Four, five . . . Madam Helen is dead because of my sister; excuse me, Karen murdered her in cold blood, framing me for the crime. Now if you would shut it, I can finish your death sentence so I can deal with that problem. Six, seven, eight . . ."

"Not Helen, God rest her soul. Your birth mother!"

"My birth mother is off somewhere in the United States or probably dead!"

"No she isn't! Michelle Cameron was the best MI6 agent that ever lived...she's not dead, she's just in hiding! And you and I are going to find her!" Out of nowhere, the sound of stomping feet began to come up the stairwell that she and Malcom previously had ventured up. Edging closer to the tower window with Justin, she glanced down at the moat surrounding the castle. It was at least a ten-story fall; a fall that would either kill them, leaving their bodies for any lingering crocodiles, or it could be the exit she'd been hoping for. She glanced at Justin as they stood mere inches from the window as Malcom advanced upon them, like a cat preying on a tiny mouse.

"Do you trust me?" she asked Justin. She didn't give him time to utter a word before she shoved him out the window. Jumping up onto the ledge, she realized that this was the second jump from a high height that she was going to make in two weeks. *I must really enjoy the adrenaline rush,* she thought, pointing her gun in the King of Crime's direction, just as Josh, Louis, and Bruce hurried into the tower with their merry band of agents. Elizabeth smiled and spoke loud and clear, seemingly setting fear in the eyes of novice agents that she saw were fresh out of the academy and were also all men, which didn't sit well with her.

"Gentlemen . . . you were just outsmarted by a woman," she pulled the trigger and shot Malcom in his right knee as she stepped out of the tower window, a shower of bullets following close behind her.

CHAPTER TWENTY-FOUR: NO HOPE

Elizabeth gasped for breath as she reached the surface and searched around franticly for Justin. How had she thought that taking this plunge was a good idea?!

"At the time, it was a good idea," she mumbled to herself. Then she felt it. The horrible pain, the horrible shooting pain shooting through her arm. Leaning against the side of the castle, she continued to tread water in the deep moat while she tried to get a good look at her shoulder. *Darn you Bruce anyhow! Or Louis. Or . . . Josh. Or that team of novices.* They'd managed to shoot a hole in her moto jacket; her favorite jacket, the gift Madam Helen gave her after she graduated the academy. She felt the hole in her shoulder and let out a hissing sound. It hurt worse than when that creep broke her arm. Her memory was suddenly fuzzy, but she was sure Scar had broken her arm three years ago when she'd given him that scar on his face. Her wound felt like a through and through; she didn't feel a bullet as much as blood seeping out of the hole in her arm, so she hoped it wasn't lodged in there and she could use her arm. At least, the conditions now weren't as bad as they had been in Greece and Bali last year during the mob war. Elizabeth heard a moan from across the moat near the drawbridge. She had to squint to see him, but the rising sun helped her make out the form of Justin; shirtless and as hot as all get out. Ignoring the pain in her shoulder, she swam over to him. Grabbing him around the waist, Elizabeth began to drag Justin and herself out onto the steep bank. It took her longer than she had anticipated, but she managed to lift them both out of the swampy moat. As she set Justin down on his back on the bank, the gorgeous man let out a soft groan.

"Justin!" she whispered. Kneeling beside him, Elizabeth placed a hand on his cheek. Justin slowly reached up and grabbed that hand.

"Your hand," he proclaimed, "is wet." He opened his eyes and smirked at her, as she blushed and secretly hoped that it was still too dark for Justin to see the bright color of her cheeks. Ignoring his snide comment, she slid her hand out from his and touched the spot where the bullet had entered his chest. He winced but made no sound as she found no bullet. She stared into his piercing eyes, making sure he was still with her.

"Can you walk?" she asked him, trying to think of a better get-away plan since she had been shot. Her head ached. She thought she could have a concussion.

"I think I can manage. I do have two legs, after all," she fought the urge to grin at him as she helped him up. His hand held onto her waist and Elizabeth drew in a quick breath and tried not to think too much into it. Back in the tower must have been the drug talking. By the sound of him now, she hoped it had worn off. She wasn't about to tell him how she felt! She'd never really felt what she felt for Justin for anyone else, and maybe she even loved him, but she could never bring herself to tell him that. Ever. Look what happened when she told Josh she loved him. What. A. Mistake. He'd kidnapped her, taken her to the U.S., proposed marriage and everything went downhill from there. *I really can pick them.* She thought as she basically dragged Justin to the drawbridge. Clumsily pushing his wringing wet body onto the bridge, she paused to focus past her throbbing arm and made it look like she was catching her breath. Biting her lip, she pulled herself up onto the drawbridge next to Justin and cautiously peered at the gatehouse. Lights out, no movement; something didn't feel right. It felt like a trap. Justin was in a sitting position and nodded as she lightly touched his knee. Having lost the gun in the jump, she was careful as she crept toward the gatehouse and a familiar smell hit her nostrils. The rising sun helped her see three MI6 fellow agents that she had graduated the academy with, who had unmistakably been dead at least two days.

Her head started to really spin. Something was very wrong with Karen's operation; perhaps she had a mole or something, but she didn't have time to think about what made Karen wrong for the position of MI6 Director at the moment. She had to get Justin to one of her safe houses that the agency hopefully knew nothing about. Glancing at the forest in front of the castle, she hurried back to Justin and helped him up with her good arm. She silently prayed that they would reach the forest before they were seen. There hadn't been any weapons in the gatehouse, so they were weaponless and the both of them needed medical attention, which they could not properly get because of the fact of who they were: the famous MIA musician and the rogue agent. As the pair reached the forest, Elizabeth glanced back at the castle and saw who appeared to be Josh standing on the drawbridge. He waved and she immediately turned her head back to concentrating on her footing. She quickly realized the position they were both in. Josh was a good shot and a bullet could be flying through the air as she thought about it. Although no bullet came, she knew there was no hope for either Justin or herself to live past the next few hours . . . but then again, what her enemies never seemed to understand was that she was Elizabeth Cameron.

CHAPTER TWENTY-FIVE:
YOU'RE STILL IN LOVE WITH MY SISTER!

Karen glared at a bandaged-knee Malcom from the chair she occupied behind her pink desk. She had dried blood on her nose from the confrontation with Elizabeth's forehead, and despite how much the sight of that blood bothered him, Malcom fought the urge to tell her to go wash it off. The last thing he needed was an upset partner covering his back; not that she wasn't upset with him already.

"So, this was your plan all along. You just wanted to get Elizabeth to help you find Michelle? You could have had the decency to inform me of your little scheme; but come to think of it, decent isn't your middle name."

"Actually, my middle name is Raymond."

"And I actually don't care. Is she really your daughter?" she asked intently, leaning toward him over her desk.

"Yes, Karen, she is. She has been since before she was born."

"That doesn't even make sense! How are you going to fix this? Since you lied to me, you *will* retrieve Elizabeth and get rid of that musician or suffer the consequences. You're dismissed."

"As you wish," he said, nearly stumbling into Josh on the way out.

"She's all yours," Malcom muttered as he limped out of the room and shut the door behind him.

"Darling!" Karen exclaimed, going over and throwing her arms around his neck. When he didn't do the same, she ignored it. When she tried to kiss him and he turned his head away, she angrily realized that hers was not the heart he desired. She released him; furious smoke threatening to pour from her ears.

"You played me, didn't you?! And for what, a shot at getting her back?! You're still in love with my sister! Come on, Josh! Don't you get it? She is over you and I'm one hundred percent positive she's in love with Justin! Not to mention you're currently with the hotter sister; but that doesn't matter, does it? Nothing I do for you will ever be enough, will it? Say something, Josh, for heaven sakes! Come on, deny it! Tell me I'm wrong," he stared at her, expressionless. She felt tears building up, but she was determined to hold them back and not cry in front of him.

"Get out. Just get out! I never want to see you again. You're not involved in this operation and if I find out you tried to cross me, I'll blow your head off. Understand?" Karen bit her lip to keep from crying. He just needed to leave so she could be alone. Josh went to the door and opened it, only to look back at her once more.

"You know I do love you, I just love Elizabeth more," Karen stared after him and as he shut the door, she let her tears fall. She stepped around to the side of her desk, picked up a pile of paper and threw them into the air in frustration. She slid down to the floor and buried her head in her arms as paper fell all around her. *I really know how to pick them. And to think I was only with Josh to get back at her; but then I stupidly fell in love with him.* Karen sobbed for quite a while until she stopped all at once and lifted her head from her arms with an evil grin on her face.

"I'm going to kill you, Elizabeth," she said out loud, "if it's the last thing I do!"

CHAPTER TWENTY-SIX: THE HIDDEN COTTAGE AND UNEXPECTED GUEST

"We can't just give up! We have to stop them!" Justin insisted as Elizabeth finished cleaning his wound and wrapped gauze around it.

"We? What are *we* supposed to do? Ask them nicely to knock it off? 'Hey Karen, I know you really hate me right now for head butting you and basically being the all-star child, but could you do me a huge favor and stop all of this rampage on London?' She'll laugh like a hyena and shoot me in the head," Elizabeth replied coldly, yanking off her jacket, frowning at the bullet hole in it and draped the jacket on the back of a chair in her cottage. They were on the very outskirts of Chelsea, in an isolated cottage surrounded by a forest of tall trees, fully stocked with medical supplies, non-perishable food, plenty of water, and of course a variety of weaponry that could hold down a small fortress. Justin had just opened a can of beans that she had found for him but glanced over as Elizabeth tried to clean her own wound with much difficulty. He left the can of barely touched beans and walked over to her.

"Let me see it," he asked, gently grabbing her wrist. Startled, she tried to pull away from him, but Justin had a firm hold. She glared at him.

"I can manage without your assistance!" she declared, trying again to tug her wrist from his grasp, but he would not release her. Justin leaned in close, and Elizabeth felt her heartbeat speed up rapidly as he pressed his lips against hers. She sighed as she put everything she had left into that kiss. Elizabeth felt the world disappear and it was just the two of them standing in the middle of the cottage. *Best kiss ever,* she declared as the Kiss of the Century ended and Justin pulled back, leaning his forehead against her own. They were breathing heavily with their eyes closed and opened their eyes at the very same moment as Justin pulled his forehead away from hers and gazed into her eyes, while Elizabeth thought she was going to melt into a puddle at his feet. His thumb gently grazed her chin as he spoke to her.

"You should let someone in once in a while," he said, taking the wet rag with soap and warm water from her hand, cleaning her wound and wrapping her arm with a bandage. When he was finished, he kissed her again but quickly this time and sat back down to eat his beans. Elizabeth shook her head and started to pace in front of the fireplace. It was chilly, but she had not yet lit a fire. She rubbed her arms and wished she had. Going to the trunk in the corner, she found a white t-shirt and tossed it at Justin, who caught it in one hand. She sighed. She wouldn't have minded him not wearing a shirt, but she really needed to concentrate. She found a black t-shirt for herself and, because Justin was in the room, she put the clean t-shirt on over her soiled one and struggled out of it, all the while not showing too much off. If Justin tried to assist her now, he would have another thing coming. That changing trick she had learned in gym class at the academy, the class that she honestly hated the most while she spent four years of her life there. Grabbing her jacket from the back of the chair, she grimaced as pain shot through her arm when she slid it into her jacket sleeve. Going over to the cupboards, she pulled out two bottles of water, placed one on the table in front of Justin and resumed her pacing after she shut the cupboard again. Justin finished his beans, put on the t-shirt and practically drained the water bottle Elizabeth had given him in one gulp.

"You're so beautiful when you pace," he said, winking at her. She blushed and kept pacing. Abruptly stopping, she turned to look at Justin with a triumphant smile on her face.

"Karen has a weakness, if she wants to admit it or not—Malcom. What a dumb partner to have! When he slips up, so does she."

"So, how do we get him to slip up?" Justin asked as Elizabeth held up her hand.

"I'm not finished quite yet. Karen has slipped up already: She's shagging Josh. We bring down Josh, we bring down Karen. Josh loves to buy really expensive random historical items; we find something that he wants so desperately that he'll leave Karen and Malcom on their own and then we got them," she finished. Justin raised his hand as if he was in a classroom and Elizabeth, was his teacher.

"Yes, Justin?" He put his hand down and winced as he crossed his arms over his chest.

"What's Malcom's slip up?"

"His downfall is me," she said as she jerked her thumb at her own self. When Justin looked confused, she continued.

"We get Josh out of the way, I go in and take out . . ." she paused to clench her teeth, "my father, and then I'll take on Karen, who won't be hard to break, and then this nightmare will be behind us," she said as Justin stood up and walked over to her, stopping mere inches apart with his arms still across his chest.

"And what of us? What's to become of us, Elizabeth?" he asked, towering over her. She gulped and decided then and there to tell him how she felt, until she saw a flash of movement out of the corner of her eye out the window. She reached for her gun that was on the counter that she had retrieved upon entering her favorite safe house. *Please let that be a deer,* she thought just as a rock type thing crashed through the window and landed by her boot. Grabbing Justin's arm, she dove under the table.

"Grenade!" she shouted, as the cottage burst into flames.

CHAPTER TWENTY-SEVEN: MARK THE ALMIGHTY

Mark grinned as he watched the cottage, or really what remained of the cottage, burn to the ground. Louis would be upset, Karen would be horrified, the crime boss would be mad, heck, even that Josh character would be upset with him because Mark was pretty sure Josh was in love with Elizabeth, but who wasn't? She was a gorgeous thing to look at, but her manners were not to his liking. Mark turned from his spot where he had been watching the flames and began to make the ten-mile hike to his car before it got too dark and before he was seen. He glanced at his watch. 3:36 PM. It had taken him under a day to figure out which safe house Elizabeth would be at. He had found it only by process of elimination, which had included an intense interrogation of Elizabeth's now former weapons supplier, which he might add made excellent boots, glancing down at the new pair he had on his feet. It had also taken him far too long to find the cottage after he figured out which one it was. Reaching for a smoke, he lit up and dialed the number that he was supposed to call when the job was finished.

"It's done," Mark said as a voice answered.

"Excellent. Make your way back here to the castle before you are missed," the voice said as Mark ended the call. Puffing on his cigarette, Mark smiled to himself as a bullet zipped through the air and struck him in the back of his head. He fell to the ground and he face planted in the forest floor, where Mark would never light up again.

CHAPTER TWENTY-EIGHT:
ALIVE AND KICKING

Elizabeth groaned before she started coughing. Quickly controlling her coughing fit, she blinked; or she thought she did. Total darkness had surrounded her, except for a thin sliver of light that looked like a square outline above her head. Only making it to a kneeling position from her current plank position, Elizabeth smacked her head on the concrete ceiling. Dizziness overcame her as she held her head in her hands.

"Here's to concussion 324," she muttered, reaching up to push on the square of concrete above her head. It didn't budge, so she sank lower and gave the square a good swift kick. It popped open and shut very quickly. Reaching up again, Elizabeth shoved the piece of cement up and to the side, causing her to briefly cover her eyes. Squinting, she figured she'd been out for a day, maybe two at the most. Glancing to her left, she saw Justin was lying on his back with his head by her knee. Groaning, he draped an arm over his eyes.

"Five more minutes, mum! I'm dreaming about sleeping!"

"If I was your mother, I'd wake you up every day with an air horn." He grinned and pretended to snore as Elizabeth hoisted herself from her "fake bottom floor," as she called it. She installed one of these in all her safe houses just in case persons that did not particularly care for her came a calling while she was there and blew up the safe house. Her arm throbbed and her ribs hurt but they were becoming more bearable by the minute. That forced rest must have done her some good.

As she stood in the ruins of her most favorite safe house, she tried to figure out who could have possibly known about her Chelsea cottage. Bruce was too dumb to figure it out. If Karen had figured it out, she most likely would've dropped a nuclear warhead on top of the cottage and leveled Chelsea, along with half of England with it. Malcom would have just sent Rock and Scar to collect her like he always did; that lazy, jolly, ugh, father of hers. Josh . . . Josh probably might have left her alone or come himself; but if he had come himself, he would have looked her in the eye before he put a bullet in her brain.

    Rubbing her temples, she made a 360 as Justin pulled himself out of the "fake bottom floor" to stand beside her. Abruptly stopping at about 250, she squinted into the afternoon sun distance, trying to make out the moving animal-like creatures a little more than a mile from them. Realizing that she was going to hurl, she grabbed a nearby stick and took off at a dead sprint toward the unknown creatures. Not sure what she would find, she was relieved to hear Justin shouting her name as she turned quickly to see him chasing after her. Spooking what turned out to be small stray dogs away, she found what appeared to be a decaying and partly eaten away human body dressed in a suit, who appeared to be a male. Kicking him over with her boot, she took one look at the man's face, turned away, and threw up what little she had in her stomach, which wasn't much as she had not eaten any beans. Wiping her mouth with the back of her hand, she composed herself just as Justin skidded to a stop beside her. Pushing the hair away from her face, she noticed then it had come out of her ponytail, and he looked her in the eye with great concern.

    "Are you alright?" Justin asked, glancing at the dead man before he looked at her again.

    "I'm fine. I just didn't expect to see Mark," she stammered, taking a spare ponytail band from her wrist to tie her dirty hair up again. Whenever she lost a ponytail band, she always mentally patted herself on the back because she always wore six extra bands on her left wrist. They honestly came in handy for so much more than just tying her hair back.

"Mark?" he asked, kneeling beside the body.

"Mark Hibbins was in my class at the academy. He wasn't always the brightest bulb in the package, so he was an office aid first and a field assistant after the fact," she replied as Justin dug a phone out of Mark's jacket pocket. Standing, he began to scroll through the call lists as Elizabeth leaned over his shoulder.

"Last call went out to a Bruce, and I quote, 'A Pain in My Bum' two days ago. Jeez, we've really been out for two days?!" he exclaimed, looking at Elizabeth, who had her mouth hanging open as she stared at the phone in his hand.

"Close your mouth, Elizabeth; although I know I look rather dashing covered in dust," Justin said, grinning as she rolled her eyes and crossed her arms.

"What happened to the Justin Max I first met? The one who didn't seem like he had a funny bone in his body?" she asked him, playfully shoving him further from herself. The smile he gave her took her breath away.

"Since I was kidnapped, shot and then drugged, then almost died, and then I told you I loved you and you didn't respond?" He wasn't smiling then, nor was smoke pouring out of his ears. He looked sad, almost broken hearted. *Tell him, Cameron. Tell him you won't be able to live without him after this nightmare is over. Tell him you've loved him since the first time you saw him live in concert. Just tell him.* Opening her mouth, her heart planned on saying all those things, telling him all of what her heart felt, but her brain decided that she wasn't going to tell him anything. Maybe it was because she was scared to admit that she was in love again. Whatever the reason, she did not have the time to get into either matter at the present moment, so she changed the subject.

"Bruce?! Why that slimy little . . . he's a dead man; or he'll wish he were dead when I get through with him! To London!" she declared as she started walking back to the crumbled cottage. Catching her arm, Justin pointed in the direction that they had been running.

"London is that way."

"Why, yes, yes, of course it is! I knew that! I'm coming for you MI6! You're not going to know what hit you!"

CHAPTER TWENTY-NINE: SHE'S DEAD?!

Karen and Malcom were strategizing when Josh strolled back into the office followed by a struggling Bruce in the iron steel holds of Rock and Scar.

"What is the meaning of this? This is a private meeting that does not concern the lot of you! And one of you I told to vanish!" Karen said, glaring at Josh.

"Upon my departure, I caught wind that this worm of an agent had gone and done the unthinkable. When I questioned the scoundrel, he did not deny it. I just thought that you would want to know," Josh replied, turning back toward the door.

"Where are you going?" asked Malcom, who was sitting in Karen's chair as she perched on the desk.

"To buy the Brooklyn Bridge. It's a private invite-only sale and I've just bid away billions of dollars," he said as his phone beeped. Smiling, he glanced at tweedle blonde and tweedle blonder. "You're looking at the new owner of the Brooklyn Bridge. I'm off to sign papers. Cheerio!" Malcom looked at Karen, a confused look growing in his old and tired eyes.

"Can he do that?" She shrugged her shoulders and looked at Bruce with a feeling of disgust, seeing as she never really liked him.

"What have you done?" She asked him as he gave her a grin that sent chills up and down her spine.

"I did it," he muttered.

"Did what? And you're mumbling. Louis mumbles quite often and I hate mumbling. Spit it out!"

"I did it!" he yelled, making Karen jump down from her

desk and walk over to stand in front of him with her arms crossed.

"You're really trying my patience. What did you do?" she asked again.

"I KILLED ELIZABETH CAMERON!" A pin could've been heard if it had been dropped. Silence doomed on for what seemed like hours until Malcom finally cleared his throat.

"Come again?"

"I highly doubt you need me to repeat that," Bruce replied as Karen said nothing. She turned and cast a blank look at Malcom before she slapped Bruce across the face. Seconds later, she slapped him again. *How dare he?* she thought. *How dare he take Elizabeth out without my order? I should kill him . . . but I'm not finished with dear old Brucey yet.*

"Throw him in isolation. I've got big plans for you, Bruce. Take him away," she ordered, waving her hand as Bruce uttered not a word as he was dragged from the room. Karen started shaking when the room emptied, leaving her alone with Malcom. *That man, that monster, that vile creature brutally murdered my sister. Well, stepsister. How could he do such a thing?* she thought as Malcom limped over and helped her to sit down on the sofa. He sat down beside her and wrapped his arm around her shoulders.

"There, there, my dear. I know you will miss your sister and our plan has changed course much more quickly, now with her out of the way faster than we anticipated, but never you fear. We'll have control of London very soon and then we'll rule side by side for the rest of our days, darling daughter," Karen jumped up from the sofa as a look of horror crossed her face. Malcom smiled and leaned back into the cushions.

"Yes, dearest. I am your father as well."

CHAPTER THIRTY:
ONE DOWN, TWO TO GO

Elizabeth smiled to herself. He'd taken the bait like she knew he would. She shook her head when she realized that she knew her ex-fiancé still all too well. He was in the past, she was totally over Josh, but was Justin her future? She glanced over at him as he looked her way at that very same moment. She blushed and looked away, unable to admit even to herself that she was indeed in love with her current charge. Justin kicked her boot lightly, bringing her out of her thoughts. They were both soaked to the bone from the downpour rain that had recently ended as the sound of Josh's chopper blades faded further and further into the distance.

"What's the plan, Agent Cameron?" Justin asked, giving her that incredible smile from the branch he sat on to the left and below hers. The great oak tree they were currently using for shelter was more than eight miles from the castle and further than she wanted to be. She wanted, needed, to know what was going on in that fortress. She hated not knowing what Karen and her, ugh, father were cooking up. She knew she was not their favorite person right now, but she had to hit them now when they were at their weakest. Josh had been the key opponent and she'd dangled a bit of historic property in front of his nose, and he'd been after it like a hunting dog picking up the scent of his quarry. He left without realizing that this was Elizabeth's play; she was telling the world that she was alive and kicking and Josh was never going to get the Brooklyn Bridge in a million years. He wouldn't figure out the scam until he arrived in the U.S., and she hoped to have taken Karen and Malcom down before he jetted back to England to stop her... or would he? Elizabeth started climbing down the huge tree and Justin followed suit; careful not to land on top of her as he jumped the last few feet to the ground.

"Now we give Malcom what he wants," she answered, talking mostly to herself, crossing her arms and turning her gaze toward the castle.

"Which is?" he asked, copying her stance.

"His daughter," Justin glared at her and shook his head as the sun began to set.

"Absolutely not! Are you insane? Wait, don't answer that. YOU ARE INSANE! What's going on inside that pretty little head of yours?" he asked, tapping her forehead with his pointer finger.

"Don't," she warned him, her eyes staring into his, challenging him to try and stop her.

"Or what? You'll kill me? Go ahead, you're not going to get a better shot. Then I don't have to watch you die in front of me. Do you even remember that Karen is after you? Hopefully she thinks you're dead, but what do you think she'll do when she finds out you're alive? Forget all about her scheme to rule MI6?"

"Actually, I've thought about it, and I think she wants to take over London. She loves power; obsessed with it. I think she wants to just do something that'll be remembered instead of being just Madam Helen's secretary and the stepsister of Elizabeth Cameron. Anyway, I think I know how to stop her, but I do need your assistance if you please," Justin sighed and shook his head.

"I will if you ask me nicely," Elizabeth rolled her eyes and tried to put on her most charming smile.

"Justin, darling, would you be so kind as to assist me in my glamourous plan to stop Karen and my supposed father from basically destroying London?" She battered her eyes the best she could and grabbed his hand. Justin smiled and shook his head.

"No," Elizabeth dropped his hand, furious.

"What? And why not?" Justin brought his face just inches from hers.

"Ask me nicer," was all he said. Elizabeth stepped back and dropped down to both knees, trying to channel her inner Sandra Bullock when her character Margret proposed to Ryan Reynolds character Andrew in *The Proposal*. She took a deep breath before she began. *I wonder if Sandra felt as silly as I do, proposing to a guy like this.*

"Would you please, please, please, with a cherry on top, help me carry out this grand plan of mine to stop a criminal crime boss and his blonde secretary sidekick?" she pleaded; a smile spreading slowing across Justin's face.

"Yes, I will. How'd you know my favorite movie is *The Proposal*?" he asked, holding out a hand to help her off of the forest floor.

"Lucky guess? Hey, wait a minute! Your favorite movie is a chick flick?"

"Yeah, so?" Justin said with a straight face.

"You shouldn't have told me that," she said with a grin, letting go of his hand. She was going to enjoy teasing him and she wasn't about to let on that *The Proposal* was indeed her favorite movie as well, and that she'd seen it in the theater twenty-seven times . . . or was that *Me Before You* she'd seen twenty-seven times in the theater?

"So, Ryan Reynolds, what's your genius plan?" She looked at his smiling face and her knees about gave way.

"Who made you Sandra?" she shot back, hugging her jacket

to her. It was chilly. Perfect. Just the way Karen hated it.

"Because I've got the better hair," he said, running his hand proudly through his filthy hair. She shook her head and turned her attention back to the castle.

"I need you to go tell your uncle that he needs to contact the Captain of the Royal Guard, Stuart Simpson. You need to tell him that Elizabeth would like him to know that she *solemnly swears she is up to no good* and get back here as soon as you can."

"What, are we wizards now?" he joked.

"I would like to be. Magic would make this so much easier," she replied seriously, giving him a quick kiss on the cheek. "I'm counting on you," she said before turning and jogging in the direction of the castle.

"I hope you know what you're doing!" he yelled after her. *That makes two of us,* she thought, as she continued toward the castle on the road that might or might not lead to her death.

CHAPTER THIRTY-ONE: DENIAL AND SUSPENSE

"You're kidding me right now. This is a huge joke! Am I being punk'd? Okay everybody; you can come out now! It's over, cameramen! You did get it filmed right, Malcom? I bet the look on my face was priceless!" Karen said, as she glanced toward the door, anticipating people rushing in to her rescue. She hoped with all of her might that what Malcom had just said was very much far from the truth.

"Your expression was indeed priceless, my dear; but despite how much you fight it, you're my daughter. I knew it the moment you contacted me about your deal in the first place. You have my eyes and your mother's attitude," he replied, his grin growing wider than she'd ever seen it before.

"That couldn't possibly be true! My father passed away before I was born!"

"That's funny, because I'm sitting right here."

"You're calling my mother a liar?"

"Why, yes, I am indeed saying she told you a great falsehood."

"You'll regret that, you old jolly man!" Karen said, as she pulled out her gun and aimed it at Malcom. For a split second, Karen thought she saw a glimmer of fear in Malcom's eyes.

"Let's talk this out, shall we?" Malcom said, his eyes growing as wide as a giant flapjack fresh off the griddle. Karen raised her eyebrows as she felt the barrel of a gun pressed against the back of her skull. Karen closed her eyes and waited for the darkness to consume her, but the foe simply spoke.

"The only person who's going to end MY father's life is me."

CHAPTER THIRTY-TWO: OH SHHH ... AND A BUNCH OF OTHER WORDS

"Nephew?! What are you doing here? How did you get here? Are you alright? Are you hurt? What happened to your clothes? Is that blood on your forehead?" Justin's uncle said, rising from his desk as his nephew entered his office through the side door.

"I'm sorry uncle Tomas; I'll tell you everything sometime soon, but at this present moment, I have no time to explain, and I need you to listen to me."

"But . . ." Tomas started.

"But nothing! I'm, uh, technically on assignment. I need you to contact the Captain of the Royal Guard, oh what's his name . . ."

"Stuart?"

"Yes! That's right! Stuart, uh, Simpson, and I need you to do it now." The older gentleman stood there dumbfounded as Justin started to yell.

"Contact him now! That woman I love is in grave danger!" The prime minister sat back down in his chair, seemingly being in no rush to do anything.

"Who? Trixie? Who bloody well cares? I've never liked her . . ."

"JUST CALL HIM!" Justin was ready to explode as a couple of security guards bust into the office.

"It's just my nephew, gentlemen. Please wait outside," Tomas said as he waved his hand to dismiss them.

"But sir, we heard shouting . . ." one started.

"It was just a disagreement. Please leave us to our private business meeting."

"Yes, sir," the security guards said, leaving the room and shutting the door behind them as Justin's uncle took his time dialing a number on the phone. *Elizabeth is counting on me, and my uncle is taking his dear sweet time . . . I wonder if he's behind my "Stalker?" No, he wouldn't do that . . . would he?* Justin wondered as he began to tap his foot until his uncle hung up the phone.

"Well?" Justin asked, crossing his arms.

"He's not in today, so you'll have to wait to speak to him when he's on duty tomorrow," Justin reached across the desk and grabbed his uncles' collar, pulling him toward him as his uncle fought hard to be rid of his grasp.

"Where can I find him?" Justin growled, cutting off the older man's air supply.

"Try . . . the pub . . . on . . . forty-third . . . street!" Tomas gasped, still trying to pry Justin's hand away. Justin let go instantly and sprinted out the door he came in.

* * *

"What was that ref?! Bloody bad call! C'mon boys! Let's go England! Jerry! Another round!" Captain Stuart Simpson waved drunkenly at the bartender named Jerry. Jerry wiped his hands on a towel and came to stand in front of Simpson as he continued to yell at the rerun match of England vs. Germany from the previous week.

"I think you've had enough, Stu. I'm going call you a cab," Jerry said as Stuart picked up his empty ale glass and threw it over Jerry's head, breaking several full liquid bottles. Jerry didn't flinch as he'd been through this "Stuart behavior" before. Stuart came in once a week to catch a rerun match and drink some ale.

"I'M NOT FINISHED YET!" yelled Stuart, leaning clumsily over the bar.

"I'm adding that to your tab after I call you a cab," Hulk-like Jerry said as Justin stepped into the crowded small London pub and walked right up to the bar and signaled to Jerry.

"Excuse me sir, I'm looking for a Stuart Simpson," he asked, and Jerry jerked his thumb toward Stuart, who happened to be seated to the left of Justin. Jerry went to refill other customers' drinks as Justin raised his eyebrow at a drunken Stuart, who turned to look him in the eye with a funny smile plastered to his unshaven face.

"He didn't serve you either, huh? Dumb barkeep!"

"I heard that! Watch your mouth, Simpson! Joy won't come pick you up if you get thrown out of here again!" Jerry yelled from the end of the bar as Stuart waved to him.

"Who's looking for CAPTAIN Stuart Simpson?" he asked, giving Justin a goofy smile as he twirled his wedding ring.

"Elizabeth Cameron," Stuart seemed to sober up in an instant as he leaned closer to Justin.

"What does she want?" he whispered.

"She has a message for you. She would like you to know that she is up to no good," Justin whispered back as Stuart shook his head and jumped off his stool.

"Always getting herself into trouble and then comes begging me to bail her out. Let's go. See you next week, Jerry!" he called over his shoulder as he headed out the door.

"You'd better behave better!" was all Jerry shouted after them as the door to the pub slammed behind them. Stuart squinted into the afternoon sun as he took his sunglasses out of his jacket and slipped them on. Pulling out his phone, he punched in a number as they started walking quickly down the sidewalk. Justin noticed that Stuart didn't seem all that drunk as he appeared to be when he had met him moments earlier. Stuart almost seemed . . . well . . . sober.

"Hello darling! How are you? Did you have a good appointment? Oh, he did? What else did he say? Everything is normal? Healthy? Good, good, that's very good. Listen, I'm probably going to be out late tonight. Elizabeth and I need to take care of something. Yes, I will give her your love. What's that? Yes, I'll ask her if she's free next week and then we'll ask. Right you are! I love you. See you soon," Stuart said as he hung up and put the phone back into his jacket.

"Where is Elizabeth?" he asked Justin as they got to his car and both hopped in.

"Breeching a castle outside of the London Wood," Stuart uttered under his breath many curse words that Justin's catholic mother had washed his mouth out with soap for saying.

"She's never been one to wait for back up. Let's go save the only woman that has ever kicked my bum . . . besides my wife." As Stuart pulled out into the afternoon traffic, Justin asked the question that had been burning up his thoughts.

"Why the *Harry Potter* reference?" he asked as the two men put on their seatbelts.

"She loves the *Harry Potter* series. She has read each novel many times over and we had frequent movie marathons during our academy days." Justin noted that Stuart was driving quite well for someone who had consumed at least two or three ales before getting into the car, but he kept his thoughts to himself.

"You went to school together?"

"She was the top student in our class. I was always right behind her in every subject, except romance. I married my wife while we were still in the academy and Elizabeth seems to have yet to find the right man. My wife, Joy and I, are expecting our first child."

"Congratulations, mate!"

"Thank you. But back to Elizabeth: if you hurt her, I'll hunt you down and break your neck." Justin looked over to see that Stuart's expression meant that he wasn't kidding.

"What are you talking about?" Justin asked as Stuart picked up speed.

"It's obvious. I could see it in your eyes back at the pub. If you're really going to try and win her over, here's two pieces of advice: her heart's been broken horribly before, so you're going to need a wire cutter to attempt to get into her heart now that she's put up a barbed wire fence." Justin waited for Stuart to continue but he was silent.

"What's the second piece of advice?" Stuart grinned as he dodged quickly around traffic.

"Good luck. You're going to need it. Elizabeth Cameron's heart isn't on her sleeve."

CHAPTER THIRTY-THREE: FALSE TRUTHS

"You just won't die, will you?" Karen said through clenched teeth.

"I'm immortal," Elizabeth responded as she took Karen's gun that she had reluctantly lowered moments earlier and put it in the back waistband of her jeans. Pushing Karen forward with her gun, Malcom grinned so devilishly that it made Elizabeth want to cringe, but she held her composure.

"What are you so smiley about?" she asked as Karen sat down on the opposite end of the couch that the jolly man occupied and crossed her legs.

"I'm so overjoyed that my little family's together!" Elizabeth raised her eyebrows and glanced at Karen, who rolled her eyes in return.

"That oaf over there says he's BOTH of our fathers," Karen said, crossing her arms. Elizabeth smirked and shook her head.

"And you believe him? I can't image why you do not remember the story of my adoption! How sad. To refresh your memory and to tell MY supposed daddy dearest all about it; I was born to a sixteen-year-old over in Colorado, U.S.A. She wanted to give me a better life, and boom: in comes an eight-month pregnant Madam Helen with little Miss Karen on the way whose father was of royal blood; Scotland's crown prince to be exact, before he went off to battle and poof! His convoy was bombed, which brings us to present day. While you are locked up this time, Malcom, a little paternity test is going to run its course and declare that neither Karen nor I are in any ways related to you, END OF STORY," Elizabeth finished as the sound of choppers were heard through the open window.

"What in the heck is that?" Karen asked as she started to stand but thought better of it and resumed her previous position on the uncomfortable couch, wondering who had picked out such a bumpy and ugly brown colored one. Oh, right: her.

"That would be the British," Elizabeth replied, a smile creeping onto her face. Malcom sighed as Karen groaned and covered her face with her hands.

"Stuart Bloody Simpson," she mumbled as the sound of firing bullets breezed through the open window.

CHAPTER THIRTY-FOUR: THE BRITISH ARE COMING!

Militia filed into the room after a few minutes of continuous gunfire. As Captain Stuart Simpson entered the room with Justin following close behind him, a formal handshake was exchanged between the Captain and Elizabeth as Elizabeth shared a small smile with Justin behind the Captain.

"You owe me now, Elizabeth," Stuart smirked as his troops handcuffed Malcom and Karen.

"How many times have I saved your bum, Captain? Do I need to bring up your stunt in Ireland last year? You know Joy is only a call away," she said, giving him a playful punch in the shoulder.

"Let's not go there," Stuart said seriously.

"Okay then. You owe me 998 more times. Not that I'm counting or anything," she said, grinning.

"Of course not," he replied as Malcom and Karen were brought before them.

"You can't do this to me, Elizabeth! I'm your sister!" Karen hissed.

"Ex-stepsister but look on the bright side: while I'm busy cleaning up your mess, you'll be staying in a hotel. A hotel with cold showers, bad food, and really, really ugly matching pajamas. You'll love it! I do believe orange is going to be your new favorite color!" Karen spit on Elizabeth's face and Elizabeth wiped spit from her cheek. She glanced at Stuart, and he nodded and spoke to his men.

"Let's give them a minute to say goodbye," Stuart turned so that his back was to Elizabeth and Karen. His men began to drag Malcom from the room, but he managed to turn and face Elizabeth one last time, that man that she would never call Father.

"I hope you'll come visit me soon, daughter. Every Sunday would be lovely to have a father/daughter chat," Malcom practically purred.

"I am not your daughter. The paternity test will prove that. Take him away, fellas."

"See you very soon, darling daughter," Malcom called as he was hauled from the room. Justin gave Elizabeth a look that said, *Don't do anything dumb* and turned his back to the two ex-sisters.

"Just tell me one thing, Karen. Why did you kill Mom?" Elizabeth asked her and Karen rolled her eyes.

"*My* mum, *my* mother; not yours. You will never have a family, you will never be anything more than that orphan brat that got everything handed to her."

"That was uncalled for!" Justin said as he spun around and headed for the ladies until Stuart grabbed his arm and stopped him.

"Wait man, this is between them."

"But . . ." Justin started, making eye contact with Elizabeth. She shook her head and looked back at Karen.

"Thanks for the parting thoughts, Karen. You always did have such a way with words." Quick as a flash, Elizabeth punched Karen's right eye, earning a howling wail as Karen collapsed onto the couch.

"How dare you?! I'm going to have a black eye!" Karen yelled through tears as Stuart tugged her off the couch.

"That's for mom. She was my mom too. Don't get into too much trouble in prison, because I'm not going to come bail you out," Stuart started to lead Karen from the room when

Elizabeth called out to him.

"Give my love to Joy, Stuart."

"Will do! She would love to see you since she's cooped up in the flat. Supper next week? I could catch a current match and you ladies could talk about whatever ladies talk about?" he asked Elizabeth.

"I'll call her tomorrow to set it up," Stuart nodded to Justin on his way out of the room.

"Good luck, mate. You're going to need it," Stuart left a silent Justin looking at Elizabeth, who seemed to find her boots rather fascinating.

CHAPTER THIRTY-FIVE: FINISHED

Elizabeth decided that it would be better if she broke the silence first.

"Thanks for coming to my rescue, Oh Sir Knight. It's such a pity I do not have a favor to give you as a symbol of my gratitude," Justin gave Elizabeth a half smile as he walked over to her.

"This was a rescue? Huh. You don't look like a damsel in distress," he replied, wrapping his arms around her.

"I could be," she whispered in his arms, as she leaned her face in closer...

"Ahem," Elizabeth pulled away quickly from Justin as Stuart's second in command stood in the open doorway looking rather uncomfortable.

"What is it, Simon?" she asked, hating the fact that she was blushing, and her fellow comrade-at-arms could tell.

"Agent Cameron, Agent Ward is unaccounted for."

"WHAT? How did he escape? I'm assuming that Stu . . . Captain Simpson had the castle on lockdown?"

"Elizabeth." Turning, she found Justin glaring at her, but she ignored him and spoke again to Simon.

"Get a team ready to go after him. He could not have gotten far! Give me five minutes."

"Yes, ma'am," the guard said and swiftly left the room.

"We need to have a discussion," Justin said, going to stand in front of her.

"What would this *discussion* be about? I need to catch Louis! He's not getting away this easily! Can we talk later? I really have to go," she replied, turning toward the door. She knew exactly what he wanted to speak to her about, but she was entirely sure she was not ready to discuss her feelings about him with him at this current moment in time.

"No! We cannot talk later!" he yelled, glaring at her backside.

"Calm down!" Elizabeth turned back to him and smirked as she crossed her arms.

"You think this is funny? You think *us* is funny?" He crossed his own arms and glared at her more angrily. She automatically put her hands on her hips to not have the same stance as Justin. It just felt too weird.

"Where is this coming from? We *barely* know each other! My job comes first, as should your music . . ."

"I do not want to discuss my music with you right now! Do you love me?" he asked sternly. Taken aback, Elizabeth swallowed hard several times before she answered.

"We barely know each other . . ." she stared. Justin had to strain to hear her response because of how quietly she said it as she looked at the ground.

"Do you love me?" he asked, much more gently than before. *Just tell him. He needs to know, and you need to admit it to yourself.* Elizabeth took another deep breath and said the first word that popped into her head.

"No," she said, as a cold silence echoed after the word and she mentally kicked herself for not telling him how she really felt, "this was an assignment; you were my charge, I protected you and did my job so we can both move on with our lives. I'm Elizabeth Cameron, an MI6 agent and I have work to get on with. This assignment is terminated and therefore over because Malcom made the whole 'Stalker' thing up so that he could draw me out into the open and present this 'daughter' ploy. You are no longer my charge, and we will have no contact from here on. Thank you for your help today and have a fantastic life," Elizabeth turned away from Justin quickly and left the room before he could see the tears that began to fall. She left him standing there not knowing that she was indeed very much in love with him as well.

CHAPTER THIRTY-SIX: THE FOOLISH

"Still no sign of Louis?" Ed asked as Elizabeth sulked into the shop after following a ghost trail for a month. She glared at him.

"How do you get your information?"

"I have my sources," Ed said, smiling. She shook her head as she answered him.

"Nope; the bugger must be a great hide and seek player. Camilla wants us to keep looking. She thinks we'll find him eventually, but I'm just not so sure. We should have found a trace of him by now!" Dropping into a chair customers used to try on shoes, she rubbed her temples.

"Camilla?" Ed asked, flipping the *open* sign to *closed* on the shop door.

"Camilla Rivers, the 'step in' Director until her Majesty chooses a new Director. Camilla's a real . . ."

"Are you sure nothing else is on your mind?" Ed interrupted, coming to stand beside her chair. Elizabeth glanced up sharply.

"No, of course not; I'm just really stressed with work. I think we should drop this Louis case and get back to more important cases; like that ruby that was taken from the British Museum two days ago. Did you know about that?" she asked him.

"Yes, indeed I did."

"Well, I'm fairly certain Edgar Von Dunn is behind it, but Camilla says finding Louis is more important. I can't wait to be elected Director! Then something might get done around here! And the test isn't back yet to tell me what I already know; that

Malcom isn't my father, but all of this waiting is so nerve wracking!" she exclaimed, getting up from the chair only to start pacing in front of it. Ed took her previously occupied chair and sighed.

"Agent Cameron, look at me." She stopped, crossed her arms, and glared at one of the few friends she had.

"What?" she exclaimed.

"Have you heard from him?" Elizabeth's heart started to beat very wildly. She had managed to forget about him . . . for a few minutes. She rolled her eyes angrily and looked at Ed.

"Are you NUTS?! He was my charge!"

"Undoubtably just . . . but, for the record, please share for the jury your true feelings for Mr. Justin Max, and none of that hog wash you fed them a mere month ago," he gestured toward his shoes.

"You need to get out more, Ed. Converse with live humans."

"Don't mock me and don't try to change the subject!"

"I care naught for Justin Max," Elizabeth said, turning a bright shade of red.

"Tell the truth," Ed insisted plainly.

"I do not love Justin Max, if that's what you're implying! He was a charge! Nothing could have happened there anyway!" Ed shook his head.

"Try again. This time with feeling!"

"Mother of Pearl! I am *IN LOVE* with Justin Max! Is that what you and your dumb jury wanted to hear, Mr. Nosey?" Elizabeth exclaimed, throwing up her hands as Ed broke into a grin.

"Precisely, and deep down that's what you needed to hear; out loud and not in your head." *Be still my beating heart . . . wait, what?* Elizabeth thought, stunned as she took several deep breaths before she spoke again.

"I've done something really, really dumb, haven't I?" she

said, looking rather sheepishly at Ed.

"Indeed, you have." She sighed, her eyes filling with tears.

"What shall I do? Perhaps he's forgotten all about me." Ed stood up quietly and placed a hand on her shoulder.

"Stop quoting *Robin Hood* and get your head in the game of life! You must figure that out for yourself and deep down, you already know the answer to that. Or you could go with plan B and be a crazy VIP fan at his downtown concert in an hour," he said, pulling a ticket from his back pocket. Really smiling for the first time in weeks, Elizabeth planted a kiss on Ed's cheek and took the ticket from him before racing to the door. She turned back just before she left.

"Thanks, Eddie! I owe you one!"

"We just want to see you happy; something we were for such a very short time," Ed whispered as the door slammed behind Elizabeth.

CHAPTER THIRTY-SEVEN: BACKSTAGE

"Thank you, London! Always a pleasure! Good night!" Justin yelled into his mic over the screaming crowd. Exiting the stage after finishing the last song of the night, he found his assistant, Jonny, waiting for him with a towel, water bottle, and a clean shirt.

"What's the occasion?" Justin asked, wiped his face with the towel, changed his shirt, and threw both at Jonny who skillfully caught them both in one hand.

"A very beautiful woman is waiting for you in your dressing room," Jonny said as Justin took a swig of water.

Justin stated walking toward his dressing room very slowly, "Claire?"

"It's not Claire," Jonny said, both men stopping short in front of a closed white door with the name 'Justin Max' at the top. Justin shook his head and looked at Jonny with sad eyes.

"Trixie? Mary Lou? I don't want to see anyone right now. I thought we discussed this," Jonny grinned and took the water bottle from Justin.

"None of the above . . . Oi! Be careful with that! It costs more than your paycheck!" Jonny suddenly took off speed walking toward the main stage, where Justin's guitar was being roughly put in its case. Justin's heart began to beat quickly as he turned the door handle and pushed open his dressing room door. Standing in the middle of the room in a knee-length blue dress with zippered black ankle boots, her moto jacket complete with the bullet hole, and her hair for once not in a ponytail, was Elizabeth Cameron.

"Hi," she said biting her lip, shifting her weight from one foot to the other.

"Hey," he said as he closed the door behind him, "You look beautiful."

"Thanks. Joy did my hair. It's her dress too, it's too small for her right now. Well, I guess it's better than being covered in dirt, huh?" she said starting to smile.

"Perhaps," he replied. A few minutes of silence passed after that where the pair just looked at each other, not knowing how to start *the* conversation of the era. Then Justin spoke first.

"What're you doing here?"

"I think that's quite obvious," she answered, rolling her eyes.

"I don't think so. You should tell me why," he said, stepping closer to the woman he knew he loved, even though they hadn't known each other very long.

"It's been a miserable month."

"Tell me about it," Justin replied, taking another step toward Elizabeth.

"I've missed you," she said sheepishly.

"And?" he asked, standing a few feet in front of her. Gulping, Elizabeth willed herself not to look away.

"You've missed me?" she guessed, as he stood a mere arm's length away from her.

"And?" Taking a breath, she held his gaze.

"I thought about you a lot, all the time in fact. I found it very hard to concentrate on much else," she told him as he closed the distance between them. Taking her in his arms, Justin looked at Elizabeth lovingly.

"Anything else?" he asked, running his thumb along her jaw. She shivered as she fell into his embrace and put her arms around him.

"I love you, Justin Max," she whispered as Justin placed a

kiss on her lips that she felt in the depth of her soul. *This is what being in love really feels like,* she thought as they broke away and Justin rested his forehead on hers.

"Nice boots," he said as they both glanced down at her black boots that might have looked similar to the ones she wore on the mission that had changed both of their lives for the better.

"Thanks. I think they go with any outfit; a necessary accessory," she said, grinning at him. He grinned back, only to quickly give her a serious facial expression.

"Don't you *ever* leave me again," he said as he kissed her a second time.

"Never," she told him in the same serious tone. He pulled away and headed for the duffle bag on the floor that Elizabeth had set her handbag next to. Kneeling, he turned his back to her before he spoke again.

"I mean it. Don't ever leave me again; I know I wouldn't be able to live without you if you left me a second time," he said as he stood up, returning to her with a small black box in his hand. Elizabeth gasped as Justin got down on one knee. Realizing he was going to utter the words that she wanted to hear, she braced herself for what was about to come next.

"Elizabeth Cameron, I love you with my whole heart."

"Well, I hope so!" she said as Justin glared at her.

"Let me finish," he said as he opened the black box to reveal the most beautiful glittering pearl ring she'd ever seen and slipped it onto her ring finger on her left hand. It bloody took her breath away. Tearing her gaze from the ring, she looked into Justin's misty eyes.

"Elizabeth, will you marry me?" Justin asked her. Without hesitation, she answered him.

"No."

CHAPTER THIRTY-EIGHT: AND THE NEW DIRECTOR IS...

"Her Majesty has made a decision," Camilla Rivers announced as she stood at the front of the conference room of the New MI6 building a few days later. The sign on the front read, White and Brown, Attorneys at Law. Elizabeth tapped her bare left-hand on the table. She knew she was the new Director by the way Camilla had welcomed her today. She would miss field work very much, but this was the role she was meant to play; Madam Helen had told her enough after she completed every mission. Glancing around the room, she saw all one hundred and forty-seven agents of the ALX location present; except Louis but including Bruce, because he'd been cleared of all charges. She'd tried to investigate that situation, but she'd been told that it was way above her pay grade. She'd get to the bottom of it once she was Director. She nodded to ten or twenty of her fellow agents that gave her thumbs up as Camilla cleared her throat.

"And the new Director of the largest branch of MI6 is . . . Bruce Bingham!" Not a cheer erupted from the roomful of agents; nor a single pair of hands clapped in congratulations. Bruce stood and smiled.

"Thank you! Thank you! I'll try to be as great a Director as Madam Helen was, rest her soul." All eyes were on Elizabeth as she quietly rose from her chair, expressionless.

"I'm sorry Camilla, but I thought you said Bruce is the new Director." Camilla looked at her with a confused expression on her face.

"He is," she replied as Elizabeth balled her hands into fists and pressed her lips together.

"And my first order as newly appointed Director of the ALX branch of MI6 is assigning you to desk duty; actually, better yet, assigning you six months of vacation time. And Elizabeth: My word is now law. You would do best to remember that." Gasps, murmurs, and boos floated about the room.

"That's not fair! She's our best agent and you bloody well know it!" an agent yelled.

"Camilla, can he do that?" An agent sitting near her asked as the room got quiet again. Camilla sighed before she answered.

"Mr. Bingham is the Director, and it would be wise for you to show him the respect he deserves." All eyes now moved back to Elizabeth, who had been silently staring at Bruce. Suddenly, she smirked.

"Huh," Elizabeth said, right before she erupted with anger. "ARE YOU FREAKING KIDDING ME?!"

CHAPTER THIRTY-NINE: THE WAKE-UP CALL

Two Weeks Later...

Elizabeth peaked around the corner into the master bedroom. She smiled to find her Fiancé still asleep in bed because it was only seven AM. She needed to be at the office by nine to continue with her latest mission's paperwork. Bruce didn't budge on the vacation time, especially when she'd socked him in the jaw in front of the whole agency, giving him the respect she thought he deserved. Then she'd gone MIA for a few weeks, leaving Justin worried sick, but Stuart reassured him that she didn't just disappear for no apparent reason: she was on a mission and would not resurface until it was completed or would call him when she needed backup.

It'd only taken her a couple weeks to track the ruby that was stolen from the British Museum by Edgar Von Dunn. She knew he'd taken the ruby for his collection, and she proved it, and then Bruce put her back on field agent duty. He said he put her back on active duty because he'd needed her there, but she knew better. He just didn't want her to sock him in the jaw again. Everyone made jokes about his bruise that didn't seem to fade for weeks after that. She was glad she'd been reinstated, and immediately took a month of vacation time with her Fiancé. That had taken persuading, but *that was another story*, she thought, turning back to her task at hand. Elizabeth raised the air horn with her newly ringed left hand and let the air horn ring loud and annoying-like. Justin jumped and almost fell out of the bed. She laughed out loud to see him jump like that. Justin shook his head and looked around the room for the culprit of the noise and glared at his soon-to-be wife.

"You'd. Better. Run," he said, pushing the covers away from him and getting out of bed.

"I am an agent of MI6, sir. We are the chasers, not the ones being chased. And besides, you wouldn't be able to catch me anyways," she said, backing out of the bedroom door. Justin took a few steps toward her, a smile slowly making its way across his face.

"Watch me," Justin said as Elizabeth took off down the stairs with Justin right behind her. Elizabeth's happy laughter could be heard throughout Madam Helen's entire household; the staff smiled as they completed their daily housework and prayed that she would be this happy forever.

CHAPTER FORTY: THE ONE THAT GOT AWAY

Late that very same night on the East London docks, another meeting took place. Two men met in the dark of the night to determine what was going to go down. The younger man spoke first.

"Thank you for meeting me. And thank you for taking care of Mark; but I do really need a couple more favors," he said, shifting his weight nervously and very much uncomfortable with the situation. He was a man of the law, and the law was meant to be always upheld. Wasn't that what he'd been taught at the academy?

"Of course, anything I can do to help ye cause," the slightly older man replied. The younger man only wore a light jacket to keep him warm, but the older man wore a baseball cap and a hood to block out his face. *I wonder why that is. It's just me he's meeting with,* the younger man thought as he continued.

"I need you to break Karen out of Alagon prison."

"Done," the older man said.

"And one more thing: I need a bomb, not a simple pipe bomb, something bigger. I need a bomb with an explosion that will demolish a building as big as, oh I don't know, Buckingham Palace."

"Certainly, consider it done; but what of Elizabeth Cameron? She's bound to know something is up now that he escaped," the slightly older man asked.

"She needs to be taken care of, but we have to draw her out, and I know just how to do it," the younger man said, reaching into his coat pocket to pull out an envelope and handed it to the older man. The older man slid a picture from the envelope.

"Three people? Three people for one person? Is this all really necessary?" The older man asked, sliding the picture back into the envelope and put it into his coat pocket. The younger man was annoyed that the older man was even capable of remorse, after all the sins that the older man claimed to have committed; but he kept his cool and explained his reasoning to the older man.

"This is Elizabeth Cameron, top agent of MI6, who's not so easily fooled. This is the way it has to be." The older man sighed.

"How much do you think she'll pay for the ransom?" The younger man about had it with the older gentleman as he began to yell at the man.

"Ransom? RANSOM? No, you idiot! Kill them! You need to kill them! I want her to know exactly who did this! ME!" Before the younger man could move, the older man had his hand around his throat.

"There be spies for Elizabeth everywhere, so I suggest ye keep ye voice down. This was such a horrible place to meet. Everyone is most likely a spy for Elizabeth down here because she saved their lives last year before the gas leaked. Now, leave everything to me. After this, Agent Elizabeth Cameron of MI6 will cause trouble for you no more. I'll be in touch," the older man let go of the younger man as he began to leave the docks. Only when the older man was out of ear shot and sight did he grab his phone from his pocket and dial his boss's number.

"Hello?"

"Our prediction was true. You need to get them out. He wants me to kill them all!"

"Slow down. Tell me exactly what went down," the caller stopped and turned to look behind him. Nothing, but he'd swore he'd heard something; a shoe dragging against the ground, a harsh breath being drawn, something. He gulped. Whatever it was, he knew he didn't have time left to waste.

"He wants me to kill the whole family. And he wants a bomb; he hinted he wants to blow up the palace . . ." the man gasped as someone plunged a knife into his back.

"You should know better than to cross me," the younger man that he'd just finished speaking to whispered in his ear as the older man dropped his phone and fell to his knees as the younger man slit his throat. The older man fell onto his stomach and stopped breathing as the younger man picked up the phone. The person on the other end of the line had been yelling, "Hello," the entire time the ordeal was going on.

"Jones cannot come to the phone right now. Please be sure to tell Captain Stuart Simpson that one of his best soldiers has been brutally murdered by yours truly." Clicking the end call button, the younger man dropped the phone into Jones's pool of blood and walked off in the direction of the city of London, whistling all the way.

THE END?